MORE THAN JUST PAPAD

Hariharan Iyer

First published in 2017 by

Becomeshakespeare.com
Wordit Content Design & Editing Services Pvt Ltd
Unit - 26, Building A-1, Nr Wadala RTO,
Wadala (East),
Mumbai 400037, India
T:+91 8080226699

©
ISBN 978-93-86487-31-5

Dedicated To

All Sindhis, who have showed the world that you don't need a state to belong to a nation.

&

All Tamil Brahmin Iyers, whose natural ability to balance the traditional and the modern makes them Indian society's unsung heroes.

PAPAD BYTES

Reactions about the book of some family members who played a key role in my real life marriage

This is not me. My personality simply does not match with Mona's. By the way, who is this Mona? Is there some girl called Mona in your life?

Rita Iyer, *my wife*

Hey Bro, is this how I laugh?

S. Ravindran, *my brother*

This is not correct. You have deleted my character from the book. After all, I had played such an important role in making your marriage happen.

Rajesh Punjabi, *my brother-in-law*

Jijaji (sister's husband), where am I in the book? After all, it was because of me that Rita and you met!

Dr. Barkha Shroff, *Rita's cousin*

After their reactions, I realised the problem. They had overlooked something important in the book – **The Disclaimer.**

Disclaimer

Though this story has been inspired by our real life marriage – my wife Rita is a Sindhi and I am an Iyer, referred commonly to as TamBrahm – this is a work of fiction and no offence is meant to any community. All characters are also fictitious. The usage of Sindhi and Tamil words as part of the story are based upon my experience with the languages and are not necessarily the correct expressions. The views and opinions about Tamil Brahmin Iyers and Sindhis as part of the story are solely the author's interpretations, and are not intended as generalisations.

Acknowledgements

➤ I thank my wife Rita for just being there in my life. Without her, this book would have never got written.

➤ Thanks also to the angel in our lives – our daughter Diksha – for showing keen interest in my writings.

➤ A very special thanks to the following people for making this unique wedding happen and thereby inspire a book years later:

  ➤ My parents Mrs and Mr KK Subramanian. My father is no more and would have been proud of my latest book

  ➤ My brother Ravindran

  ➤ My late father-in-law Mr Gul Punjabi, one of the nicest people I have met in my life

  ➤ My mother-in-law Mrs Usha Punjabi

  ➤ My brother-in-law Rajesh Punjabi

  ➤ My wife's cousin Dr. Barkha Shroff and Dr. Barkha's parents Mrs and Mr Kamal Batheja. They were instrumental in making our marriage happen.

➤ The other people I would like to thank are: My cousin Durga and my wife's cousin Ritu for their valuable inputs.

➤ BecomeShakespeare.com for publishing this book.

And of course all you readers.

Special Dedication

I dedicate this book to Mr Kamal Batheja, whom we fondly called Kamal uncle. He was looking forward to the release of this book and teasingly said he would like to be the chief guest at its launch.

He passed away last year. The chapter 'My Life's Most Important Interview' is a fictionalised account of uncle's real interview of mine before giving my in-laws his go-ahead.

Truly miss Kamal uncle.

CONTENTS

ROASTED PAPAD

Oohs! And Aahs!

O n a Sunday when people look forward to their post-lunch afternoon nap, I decided to provide a breaking news to my parents which could potentially disturb their night's sleep too.

"I never thought you would do this," my mother said with agony in her voice, stressing on the word 'you'. I had just broken news about my love for a Sindhi girl and my intentions to marry her. "Wait till I make you repeat this sentence more often," I said to myself, swallowing the angst that naturally emerged because of my mother's reaction.

My father, sitting next to her, looked intently at me with an expression of shock in his face and eyes. He had two sons, Krishnan – my elder brother by four years – and me, Srikkanth. His dreams of getting home a typical Tamil girl who would serve him hot piping filter coffee every morning and prepare wonderful South Indian delicacies seemed to be coming crashing down. These were the thoughts I think he was occupied with, and so he asked, "What do they eat? Mutton and chicken?" "They also eat dal, rice," I said matter-of-factly.

Just then the door bell rang. I got up to open the door if only to give the simmering tension a break. It was my brother. He sensed there was something amiss in the atmosphere. But even before he could ask what had gone wrong, my mother said with a very sad expression on her face, as if to attract the most possible sympathy from her elder son, "Your brother has fallen into bad ways. He says he wants to marry a Sindhi girl. What will happen to our culture?" My brother seemed more amused than stressed by the situation. He always liked variety in his life. His restless nature always searched for the incredible in life. But his variety was restricted to the different types of Tamil girls he fantasized about marrying one day.

His greatest fantasy was to have his wife feed him curd rice in the night and then take her to bed and feed himself on her. But I seemed to have stretched his love for variety beyond the borders of Tamil Nadu. He immediately reacted: "Oh....Sindhi *saaeen*...." (it was lost on him that Sindhis reserved the word *saaeen* – meaning a respected person – for men) and started laughing like a maniac. None of us found the occasion right for a joke and looked at him with disdain. He however was so full of his own laughter – some people love their own voice, but my brother loved his own laughter, as after all mostly he was the only one laughing after he had cracked a joke – that he ignored our dirty glances and posed the ultimate question of the day: "What's her name?" "Mona," I said. Incredibly, my brother found another opportunity to laugh. "So she is the secretary of the Hindi film villain Ajit?," and started laughing loudly again. "Shut up and sit down. Don't you have any sense at all? We are discussing an important issue here and you find it funny?," my father shouted with some fury in his eyes. The mood was definitely not conducive for a peaceful afternoon sleep.

The timing of my announcement was not lost on anybody. Just the previous day, my parents had returned from Nagpur after attending my cousin's wedding who had married a German girl Anne. My parents that Sunday morning were all praise for Anne who had dressed in traditional Indian clothing and gone through each and every excruciating ceremony with a smile on her face, whereas, it seems it was my cousin who kept cribbing through the ceremony calling our tradition archaic and out of touch with times. My brother and I could not attend this historic trans-national wedding due to our work commitments. I suppose more sparks would have flown at me if my cousin Raghu had not transcended nations. After all, I was staying within limits – inside the country – and so it could not be termed as "selling yourself to foreign powers" as my father, if he had been a politician, would have termed.

Looking at me intently, my father continued, "And what is her surname?" "Punjabi," I said. "She is a Sindhi or a Punjabi?" "A Sindhi Punjabi," I said, adding to his irritation and confusion. "Hello! she can either be a Sindhi or a Punjabi. How can she be both?," my father asked, with irritation oozing out of his every pore. "No. She is a Sindhi, but her surname is Punjabi," I clarified.

"Sindhi or Punjabi, she is not from our community," my mother said, breaking her silence, but also breaking into light measured sobs, making me wonder at the authenticity of her pain, further instilling in me the feeling that she was out to grab sympathy that afternoon, if not sleep. "Where does she live?," my father asked. "In Chembur." "What does her father do?" "He is a businessman, a self made man. Her mother is a housewife and she has a younger sister Pinky. Her father came to India with his parents after partition." "Oh! she is a Pakistani, haan? Ha, ha, ha, ha," my brother took off again. "Hey! *konjam chumma iru daa (please keep quiet)*," my father pleaded with him in Tamil. "Where did you meet her?," he asked me. "We work together," I said. "I see," he said, his expression suggesting that while I did go to work, I was at work on something else apart from work. My father, a traditional loyal employee, could never fathom why people indulged in 'immoral' and 'time-wasting activities' like 'love affairs' at the workplace.

A brief pause followed. My parents had had enough. "We will discuss this later," my father said and got up to leave for his afternoon nap. My mother followed suit with an expression that suggested only Tamil girls had a right to marry a nut like me. My brother stayed on to find out more about Mona, or at least, that's what I thought.

"What is Pinky's age?," he asked with mischief and a sense of expectancy about to pounce out of his eyes. "Sorry Bro, she can only be your kid sister. She is eight years younger to Mona." "How old is Mona?" "Three years less my age," I said, a bit irritated. "Ah....

which means Mona is 27, and Pinky is........" "Mona and Pinky. Are they Sindhi Christians?," my brother asked. "No." Then why such names? "It is common amongst Sindhis," I said. "Oh....," he said, and got up to go out to meet his friends, more out of disappointment regarding Pinky's age than anything else.

Simultaneously At Mona's House

"Nallo cha aahe (what's his name)?," Mona's father asked her in Sindhi, in a tone that suggested how dare you say whom you want to marry when that is solely my prerogative. "Srikkanth," Mona said. "Srikkanth what?" "Ah...something, something, then Srikkanth something," Mona said, bypassing everything in the name that was not Srikkanth. "What kind of a name is that?" "His name is Srikkanth Iyer, but he also attaches initials before his name and his surname after his name. His name is KS Srikkanth Iyer."

Actually, she was just summarising my full name: Kaladaikurchi Subramanian Srikkanth Iyer. Now let me explain this. Tamilians believe in giving their identity a completeness. Kaladaikurchi is the name of my ancestral village, Subramanian is my father's name and Iyer indicates that we are Shaivites – worshippers of Lord Shiva.

Actually, the name I was given at birth was Vishwanathan. Mr Vishwanathan was the elder brother of my grandfather and I was born a few months after he had passed away. Basically tradition is that a new baby – be boy or girl – has to bear the name of the grandfather or grandmother to ensure continuity. My brother had already used up my grandfather's name and therefore it was not available for my consumption. But then why was I also called Srikkanth? Oh! that's because as my mother once told me: "We can't show disrespect to your father's uncle by calling you by his name."

I was convinced that all Tamil Brahmin Iyers were born intelligent, but education spoilt them. That's why I did not manage to go beyond graduation, and that too after ATKTs in my second and third year BCom. Now you know why my mother stressed on 'you'. In a way she was paying me a compliment. She thought even Tamil girls would not be interested in me. Then how come I managed to 'trap' a rich Sindhi? (By the way, most South Indians think most Sindhis are rich and most Sindhis think most South Indians are educated!).

But most importantly, we are supposed to be Tamil Brahmins, Iyers at that, the twice born – a term reserved for men. I always wondered why we were referred to as twice born. I figured that out in my own unique way by concluding that given the length of our names it would take at least two attempts to produce us! The real reason of course is that brahmins in general, post their thread ceremony, are referred to as twice born.

"How do you know him?," Mona's father asked her in a stern voice. "We work in the same office." "I told you not to send her to work. See what she has done," her mother responded with sobs. This was the first time in her life she had defied her husband in front of her children. After all, culture and common sense are more important in such critical junctures of life than the practice of the archaic habit of *pati-vrata* (*a Hindi term for husband-worship. "Tun chup kare veh (you keep quiet),"* he said. "I am talking to her."

"From tomorrow you are not going to office. My best friend Mirchandani and his family don't want their daughter-in-law to work," Mona's father thundered. "What?," Mona screamed – even I could hear it 20 km away in Mulund, a Mumbai suburb.

My girl friend was not like her mother. She was neither a *pita-vrata* (*father-worship*), nor was she likely to be a *pati-vrata*. "It is my life and I will decide whom I want to marry. And what made you think I will marry that Mirchandani uncle's duplicate son from Ulhasnagar?" Later when she shared this incident with me, I told her tongue-in-cheek that I was not aware Ulhasnagar was famous for inventing human duplicates too.

Legend has it that 'duplicate' products thrive in Ulhasnagar, also referred to as India's USA (Ulhasnagar Sindhi Association). For the uninitiated, Ulhasnagar is situated on the outskirts of Mumbai and would have been a frontrunner for being made the capital of Sindhisthan, if such a state had existed. Post partition, many Sindhis were put up in refugee camps in Ulhasnagar and Chembur (in North East Mumbai), and therefore both these places have more than a fair share of Sindhi population.

"Okay, you need not marry him. But you are not marrying a Madrasi either," her father said, and got up in anger and left the room, leaving a fuming Mona, a sobbing mother and a 'what's-the-fuss-all-about' sister for company.

In Office The Next Day

This was definitely not the same old boring Monday morning. After sparks had flown at both our homes, we were quite excited about meeting at the office cafeteria first thing in the morning to replay the previous day's screenplay. I tried speaking to Mona the previous night, but she said in a hush, hush tone when I called: "Sri, can't speak now. My parents are sadder than how they would have felt if I had died," and disconnected. So I simply messaged: "Meet you at the cafeteria at 8 am sharp tomorrow."

At my place, my brother had kept the proceedings alive even as the rest of us tried to bear the silence around the dinner table. As he pushed into his mouth another ball of rice with curd and a touch of sambhar, he blurted out: "So Sri, you love a Sindhi papad haan?" "They are more than just papad," I said, as I ironically picked up another fried papad from the table, broke some part of it, mixed it with my curd rice and put it in my mouth. As I ate silently – I mean the mind was making multiple noises, but my mouth was opening only to eat and not to talk – I wondered at the great Indian stereotypes. Sindhis are strongly perceived as a papad-eating community. But I wondered why

South Indians were never perceived like that, as in my experience no meal in an average household in the south is complete without *appalaam* (papad that is)!

The next morning I arrived at the cafeteria at 7.30 itself. The housekeeping staff tried keeping me out of it for a while, but I insisted on sitting at our favourite table and promised to co-operate by lifting my leg whenever a mopper threatened to molest it. Usually Mona and I met on Sunday evenings and enjoyed each other's company. We now felt it was time to take our year-long courtship to the next level and therefore decided to use up the last Sunday to provide some food for thought for our family members. However, we realized that it had seriously interfered with their thought for food that day. The food never tasted more bland than on that day. The cooking was not bad, but they could not stomach what we were cooking in our lives.

Mona arrived unusually late by 15 minutes. She came into the cafeteria almost running as she hated being late and could not tolerate late-comers. "Sorry Sri. I actually sneaked out of the house as my father did not want me to step out ever again without his permission. I got out just as he entered the bathroom.

But I am afraid he might come to office today and create a scene," she said, even as she continued to breathe heavy. "Relax darling, sit down," I said.

Mona, as usual, was wearing a half-sleeve shirt and a trouser. She was unlike any average Tamil girl. She had a bob cut, was boyish and bold. Tradition to her was what was practised yesterday, not what was practised for generations. She was milk white, against my reluctant brownish-blackish complexion, and her height was 5'10 against my 6'1. She looked smart and I often tried looking smart, but falling way short of my own expectations. She was dynamic and outspoken, and I was measured in my words. Her father owned an electronics goods showroom and was also a player in the stock market; my father was a cost accountant and worked in a shipping company for the last twenty five years. So as such, nothing was common between us. I really was no match for her – at least that's what my envious colleagues, who too had a keen interest in Mona, believed. Despite the contrasts the belief 'marriages are made in heaven' seemed to be playing out. We loved each other and wanted to get married.

My cousins often told me, "Hey Sri. Would love to marry a North Indian yaar. But we are told North

Indian girls don't marry South Indians as they are fair and we are black" – another stereotype that NIs are white and SIs are black.

Mona was pretty, but not so beautiful that you would want to take serious *panga* (Mumbaiya Hindi for conflict) with your orthodox parents. I always wondered what attracted us to each other. We both worked for a life insurance company. I had joined as a sales manager and was now a senior sales manager, and she was head of customer service in our branch. I was an above-average performer despite my perceived reticence and she was seen as a dynamic person with a loud voice. So ideally we should have swapped roles, as our personalities were suited for each other's job profile. But then, isn't marriage a synergy between two opposites?

"Sri, I am seriously worried," Mona said, interrupting my gaze upon her and my train of thoughts. "My parents are extremely upset. They could have tolerated a Sindhi from Pakistan, but they are unable to tolerate a Madrasi from India." "Relax," I said. "We'll find a way out," and ordered for coffee for two. "What about your parents Sri? What was their reaction?," Mona asked anxiously, hoping that at least one set of parents would stand by us. But what she heard next did not add to her optimism in any way. "Well, they too would have preferred a Tamil from Pakistan, but not a Sindhi from Hindustan. However, I don't think they make Tamils out there," I said, trying to humour her with a cheeky smile. "Sri, you find this situation funny? Come to my home. I don't even know what awaits me when I get back today. Knowing Mom, she would be planning to call a few elderly 'counselors' to my home for high tea today to drill some sense into my head." "No," I am not finding it funny, I said. "I am just trying to de-stress each other, as you know another stress meeting awaits us at 9.30 today – the great Monday morning huddle, or should I say hurdle?" "Yes, I agree, we need to de-stress before that."

We quietly drank coffee for some time, wondering what to do next. Soon we realised a few of our colleagues had started making a beeline for the cafeteria. Our Boss, the branch manager, Mr Siddharth Pandey, also arrived for his customary morning coffee. Siddharth, six feet tall, was a dynamic young branch head, aged only 30. He however carried a balding hairline and darkening complexion, caused by the stress of his sales achievements. Prior to joining our company four years ago as a sales manager, he had sold vacuum cleaners door-to-door. I was 30 too, but was only senior sales manager; obviously, I was not as dynamic and sales- oriented as him! "Sri, I will come with you one day on the field and teach you and your agents how to sell life insurance. My record in vacuum cleaner sales is yet to be broken in my previous organisation," he would boast. He repeated this statement once a fortnight, but in the time that we worked together, he never once stepped out of his air-conditioned cabin. I wondered whether his vacuum cleaners had in-built Acs, which made him 'cool'. But he had good leadership qualities, and knew how to get reasonably good work done even from an unnatural sales guy like me.

"Hi Boss," Mona greeted him with a smile. "Hi both," Siddharth said with a tweaky smile. Like on all Mondays, there was a spring in his steps that day too, as his moment of glory was just a few minutes away. He would be the General in the great Monday morning hurdle (sorry, huddle) where the entire office would be a witness to a liberal dose of expletives inspired by below-par sales numbers for last week. Even if we met targets, he would use expletives and boast: "You should be an overachiever like me."

Both Mona and me tried to put our best faces forward, moved towards our respective work stations and then proceeded to the conference room for the office meeting. In meetings or in office we kept our distance from each other and communicated professionally. Of course, we kept messaging each other through the day to stay in touch and get updates. The whole office was aware of our affair, but appreciated our mature and professional conduct. The company had a policy that husband and wife could not work in the same office or the same department. So one of us had to move out post marriage, either out of the company or to another office. But after the previous day's Earth-shaking reactions from both sides, that seemed a long way off.

The Oohs! and Aahs! had just started.

SWEET PAPAD

How Mona And I Rose In Love

Mona had joined our office a year-and-a-half back. She had joined us from a bank and gained a more senior profile. Our office in Andheri, Mumbai's western suburb, was one of the performing branches in the country and so the customer traffic and business volume were pretty high. This meant she had a more-than-decent workload. That kept her in office till at least 8-8.30 pm almost daily, and on month-ends till midnight. She was the most sought-after person on month-ends and on other days the most discussed about. In short, she was always a part of the office's daily consciousness.

On the day she joined, Siddharth introduced her to each one of us personally. When I shook hands with her, I intuitively felt she was a warm and kind person at heart and said so in so many words. "How do you know?," she asked. "Well, an old college trick," I was about to say, but Thank God, refrained myself. "Just feel that way," I saved myself. But that kind of remained with her and I realised how easy it was to floor women if you were sincere in your praise. It is another matter that most women think that most men are sex-starved and use flattery as the only resort to get access to them. All women, irrespective of caste, creed, religion, I have discovered, are flattered by flattery even if they know it is just a tried and trusted gimmick the naughty boys of this world use on them. But they don't so easily accept your proposal, and why should they? After all, the demand-supply equation is always in their favour. They are always in demand and the men, irrespective of their genre, are always in high supply.

A few days later as I was sitting alone in the cafeteria eating a sandwich like a famished salesman, Mona picked up a cup of coffee and sat next to me. "Tell me, why did you say I was kind hearted?," she wanted to know. "Because I felt so," I said. "But how can you say that without even knowing me?" "You don't have to know people for too long to form an opinion," I said. "But there has to be some reason." "The warmth in your hands conveyed that." Mona now really got irritated. "You mean to say any woman whose hand is warm is kind hearted,? she asked, lightly banging the coffee mug on the table and spilling some of it. "What rubbish!" "Why don't you just take my statement on face value,?" I protested. "No, I can't. I need some logic," she said and got up to leave as a customer was heard making a scene at the front desk. "Catch you later Sri."

After she left, even I wondered why I had said that. I was not the type who flirted around. After all, I was a TamBrahm Iyer rooted in tradition, whose first kiss is mostly on the first night, that too after furious rehearsals in front of the mirror for a few weeks preceding the D Day, or should I say the D Night? Of course I am not counting the numerous kisses TamBrahm Iyers plant on various beautiful women as a child. Don't understand why we kids ever wanted to grow up, given the luxury of the number of kisses we were privileged to receive and give. In fact, women would say, "Come baby, give me a kiss."

I had had a long day in the field and was feeling tired, so couched myself in the cafeteria a while longer. But Mona's question started gripping me. I wondered more intensely why I said that, and in any case why is she so concerned? When will women stop doubting men, I wondered. The whole debate of why I said what I said seemed frivolous to me in light of the numerous national issues demanding attention, like why such a large number of people in our country were under insured, how would middle class and poor families pay up for the high cost of their children's education, inflation, etc. But little did I realise that day that many profound love stories have their origin in seemingly frivolous arguments or discussions.

But one thing was for sure; from the moment Mona arrived on my table, I started feeling more relaxed and energetic. The sun bath I was subjected to for the better part of the day had been replaced by a cool feeling of warmth. There were other lady colleagues in my office with whom I shared a table often, but never ever did I really feel so refreshed. In fact, in case of some, I felt de-energised in their presence, as they mostly cribbed about the Mumbai climate, their mother-in-law, the rush in the local train, their clients or agents, or anything that would provide an opportunity to give vent to their frustration.

But as the days and weeks passed, Mona to me seemed different. She always had a smile on her face – a professional requirement maybe, as she was into client servicing. She seemed to be more comfortable keeping the women away and spent most of her off-work time in office with me at the cafeteria, if I was around. Otherwise, as my good friend and colleague Prashant pointed out to me one day: "Sri, she normally stays aloof when you are not around. With others she is not so comfortable. You know about our desperate friends in sales. They don't waste any opportunity to get close to beautiful women." We both giggled in agreement. But even my great observer friend could not have guessed that Mona had started liking me. Even Mona, I am sure, had no clue about this law of attraction in action.

From about twenty five years of age I had started thinking about my marriage, more as a philosophical thought than as anything substantial. But as I looked around, I felt the inevitability of marriage in our lives. India is a fascinating country, or some would say a ridiculous country, where marriage is at the center of the decision-making process in our life. If a newly wed couple are blessed with a baby girl, they almost instantly become conscious of a marriage-related expense which is at least a good twenty two years away. If it is a boy, they are concerned about his good education, so that he will get a good wife.

Often, for most Indians, I felt, marriage was the sole purpose of existence. I wondered if there were only two reasons for this: one, both men and women in our country had irrepressible libidos, and therefore marriage as an institution offered them the best possible channel for sexual expression, and two, it was a strong conditioning that had travelled through generations. Conditioning can be both good and bad. On the outside at least, India seemed to me at that time to have benefited from this conditioning in terms of providing family and social stability. I had not yet got deeply involved with Mona to be able to reason anything else.

But marriage was unlikely to happen for me anytime soon, as my brother was yet unmarried and the years that kept adding to his life seemed to be taking him further away from the nuptial knot. But I always found his optimism amusing. When he was younger he wished to marry somebody older than him, but as he grew older, he wanted somebody much younger than him. So when the Mona tornado hit my parents that Sunday, at one level they felt let down that I had finally managed to disturb the chronological order in the family.

The fact that my brother came before me did not necessarily mean I'll find a girl for myself only after him. I could go one step ahead here, I thought, and have kids fast so that when he gets married and has children, they will call mine as *anna* (elder brother) or *akka* (elder sister), depending on whether I fathered a male or a female child, or both. The bad thing about chronology is that you don't know why you did not deserve to be the elder one, but the neutral thing about chronology is that as a process it does not interfere with people who have bet their life on initiative, and initiative I had taken.

I always used to wonder what kind of a wife would suit me. After all, if having a wife was so central to existence, then I ought to introspect deeply. Actually, as I set about the thinking process, I felt I was asking the wrong question. I should rather be asking what kind of women would find me suitable? Because, having observed my mother and several other lady relatives from close quarters, when it came to understanding women, it was an exercise in futility. For one thing, I never understood why a good mother became a terror the moment she also became a mother-in-law. In other words, I could never understand why one woman was the other woman's, or in some instances, many other women's greatest enemy! In a country which prides itself on its diversity of culture and behaviour, one behaviour cutting across religion, caste, creed, state, community never changed, and that was the mother-in-law-daughter-in-law equation. So much for national integration! But I also observed women often saying only a woman can understand another woman. At such times I used to wonder whether in a mother-in-law-daughter-in-law relationship, one of them perceived the other to be a man. If only a woman can understand another woman, then for God's sake why do they fight?

Interestingly, I never heard anybody say a man is a man's greatest enemy. I quickly figured out why – because a man does not require another man to destroy his citadel of peace, he is quite capable of doing it himself. That's why you will find a newly-wed Tamil girl often tell her mother, "My husband is just like *Appa* (father; in Tamil, mother is addressed as *Amma*), I mean my *Appa*, not his *Appa*." Then the mother would respond with a halo around her head: "Don't worry, he will also be the same. All men are the same." Of course, in the eyes of all women, all men are the same – in this too, national integration is achieved without much ado. But this only shows that women don't look for their father in their husband, they happily find their father in their husband. That's why they don't miss their father much after marriage – or at least my experience suggests they don't speak too much about it – but they certainly make a huge noise about missing their mother. Quite obviously, because while the husband fits in as a father too, the husband's mother is hardly likely to treat her daughter-in-law like her daughter. Uff! It's so complex.

Well, I continued to ponder upon the kind of person I would end up marrying. A few questions crossed my mind: What will she be like? How will I know this is my wife? How will the cosmic timing match when both of us will know we are made for each other, and the marriage, which was made in heaven, will finally be confirmed on Earth? I found the whole process complicated, and at times discussed this with my parents over dinner. But my father and mother did not find it so complicated. "In our days," my father once said, "our parents used to select the spouse for us. I saw your mother properly only on the marriage day." "Too risky," I thought, but did not dare say it. Actually, it is a nice, simple process. From generation to generation, parents select their children's bride and bridegroom and the undoubting children just keep moving on in life. I am sure such a process would create no complications like the one Mona and I had landed all of us in.

But reflecting on what my father said, I felt it was a feudal process. I should have the right to select the person I am going to sleep with and live with for the rest of my life. But my 'liberal' father did add: "Things have changed now. Children select their own spouse and parents also need to change with the times." But when the time came for him to live his statement, I felt he was mentally running away from reality.

Of course, I fantasised about who my wife would be and if it was an arranged marriage – I couldn't quite think somebody would fall in love with me, after all I felt I had little going for me in terms of my appearance and personality, as I was tall, dark, but not handsome; but yes, I fulfilled one very important South Indian quality, I had a 'steady' and 'confirmed' job – how I would spend the first night with a dusky, heavy sari clad lady decked up with flowers all along her long hair with heavy jewellery decorating her ears, neck, nose and forehead. I wondered whether before mating time, the time would have passed, and instead of a fascinating first night, we would be staring at a first morning, with all relatives searching you and your wife with eyes that would resemble a CT scan, looking for marks that would suggest that the two bodies had really met and not slept off due to the sheer exhaustion of marriage.

Having attended a lot of Tamil weddings, I realised why couples felt less excited soon after their marriage. Traditional Tamil weddings take a lot out of you – the sheer exhaustion of the marriage process takes the sting out of you. It takes at least three days of various pujas, rituals and change of clothes before the *mangalsutra (a holy thread which is an integral part of Hindu marriages)* is finally tied around your wife's neck and we are declared as man and wife. But then follows a series of full body-stretched *namaskars* (prostrations) to the elders to seek their blessings with the two-and-a-half kg garland still hanging around our necks. I love the North Indian way of seeking blessings though. You just bow down to touch their feet and most of them are kind enough to stop you mid way, give you a hug and also place some money in your hands because of your sincere labour and for the fact that you are a son-in-law. The money adds to the incentive of going on a feet-touching spree. It energises you.

But in case of the full body-stretched *namaskar,* all you receive for your labour is an abstract sense of energy flowing from the outstretched right palm of the elders, a few pieces of dry yellow rice showered on your head, and possibly seeds of a future back problem. I think it is more tough on the ladies, as they not only have to carry the garland around their neck, but also the heavy artillery called sari and the accompanying jewellery. The men are mostly bare bodied during the ceremony and after, maybe to give the girl's side an insight into the titillating hair the wife will be in possession of for the rest of her life. But Thank God! they allow you to wear a *veshti* (*dhoti – a white cloth which is tied from the waist and covers the legs*), never mind even if you keep it tightly fastened with a belt.

Of course, the climax of the wedding process – the evening reception – is the most tedious, especially if you hold a reception for about 500 people in Chennai which celebrates only three seasons – hot, hotter and hottest – and that too in a non-AC hall wearing a full length suit and a tie hanging from your neck like a hangman's noose.

You and your wife, who, having effortlessly moved from one heavy artillery dressing to another, would be standing, smiling, greeting and continuously wiping pouring sweat for over three hours before being allowed to sit down, take a breath and have dinner. I wondered why men were not allowed to stand bare bodied with the very comfortable *veshti* to cover their morality during their marriage reception too. By the time such receptions get over, the much fantasised about 'climax' on the first night gets pushed deep into the inner recesses of your subconscious.

What also used to frighten me was what one of my male cousins shared post his marriage: "Sri, the moment I was all set for attack after finally having some privacy, my wife dropped a bombshell. She said she had prayed to her family deity that she would consummate the marriage only after she got her husband along for *darshan* (holy vision). So I would have to wait for another seven days, as her family also wanted to accompany us and they were unable to come for the next seven days. But she was considerate enough to say we could proceed on our short honeymoon before that." I was aghast, wondering at the difference in perception regarding activities while on a honeymoon between a man and his wife; while the wife was quite content to go sight seeing and clicking photographs with her new-found permanent prey, the husband all the time had been researching and planning moves on how to get his wife to participate in his sexual pyrotechnics.

When my cousin shared this with me, I wondered whether all going-to-get-married-to-each-other couples should undergo a sexual education course before they took the plunge into wedlock, or should I say bedlock! The whole issue of getting married to a typical Tamil Brahmin Iyer girl seemed quite complicated, and I too was a victim of stereotypes. I imagined my wife would be dusky in complexion with long hair, clad in a heavy artillery sari. This is despite the fact that I had so many girl relatives who were bright coloured, had shorter hair and could also offer a lesson or two on modernism to women from other communities.

But there was another reason why I felt getting married could prove to be pretty complicated - my inimitable brother. A Bcom by education and a copy writer by profession, my parents believed he had a set job and our 1 BHK house could be modified into a 2 BHK house to provide him and his wife with some privacy. A middle class dream could well be getting fulfilled.

We Tamils have a formula for happiness that most manage to practice with relative ease. It goes like this: Get a degree from a good university, settle into a job – preferably a government job – get married, take a housing loan from the employer, keep paying EMI till you retire, pass on the formula to your children – have two, not more, not less; the elder one should be a girl, as girls can take care of their cantankerous younger brother better (of course you can't always get the chronology and the preferred sexes right, but you can pray at least) – take a handsome PF and gratuity home post retirement and live the rest of your life happily playing with your grandchildren, and yes, the house for which you were paying EMI all your life, is finally yours and only yours.

My father, who wanted both of us to be accounts wizards like himself – at least he thought he was one, but that never reflected in our economic status; he worked hard to help his employer make a lot of money, but always advised us to save more – was sorely disappointed when, despite our best efforts to pursue tradition, failed to ignite enough interest within ourselves to be able to crack open the mystery behind the questions that would have qualified us as cost accountants. We understood the meaning of cost to company better than the terminologies that made up a course on cost accountancy (yes, my brother and I did find our synergy occasionally, and our Bcom degrees was a lifelong one). Amazingly, the formula worked till such time characters like my brother and me stepped on to Planet Earth, apparently in a bid to take charge of our elusive destinies.

Looking at our grades in school and college, my parents often lamented, "God only knows how these two landed on our laps. Look at Sridhar (my father's elder brother's son), he always comes first in class and surely will get a good job and a good wife. Wonder what is the future of these two?" They wouldn't have budgeted for Mona of course when they made that statement. Our vacations were normally spent listening to this statement often. But my mother sometimes let her optimism shine through and let her guard down in front of her disciplinarian husband and say tongue-in-cheek: "Don't worry if a person like you can get a good wife like me, they will find their match too."

But getting married for me was not going to be so easy. My brother had a chronological advantage which he was not leveraging substantially, which meant I had to wait till he tied the knot so that I too could break my bachelorhood. Krish, however, was not too keen on tying the knot as he felt he had not yet settled down professionally, even though he was about to cross the danger mark of 35, by which time you excepted him to have not only got married, but also have a son/daughter, with a second one on the way. But as the situation had it, we kept going from home to home of different prospective girls, liberally gobbling up the *bhajji* (fritters) and *kesari* (sweet dish made of *suji*) which were served at each of these 'girl-seeing ceremonies'. In our community, as part of the arranged marriage process, there is this tradition of the boy's family visiting the prospective girl's family after the horoscopes had matched. These visits continue till such time both the boy and girl either don't say yes together, or one, or both of them reject the other. Krish went through the motions which meant even if a 'suitable' girl did come across, he would find some excuse to not go ahead. He hated this bhajji-kesari eating process – and me too – but we kept going through the rigmarole so as not to upset our parents. My breaking news about Mona however did take the attention away from Krish for some time.

The Turning Point

The turning point in our relationship came during a heavy downpour on a particularly monstrous monsoon day in Mumbai. It was a normal day at work. However, things quickly changed by 4 pm when the heavenly gates opened their doors and torrential rains lashed Mumbai city. People in Mumbai are quite cool about the monsoons as they are used to heavy rains; in fact, they enjoy and look forward to them. But on this day, by 6 pm, news came that there had been a cloud burst and the entire city had hurtled towards a shutdown. We all quickly tried to move out of office and reach home. However, when few of my colleagues and I ventured out of the office to find a transport to get home, we were stunned to see the rush of water in the building compound. It seemed the Ganges in its full fury had come visiting us. We realised we could not get home at that point and turned to get back to office. We had to wait for the rains to subside.

In office we realised the mobile network had collapsed and so only had the landline connections.

There was total panic in the air. After a while I noticed our Boss Siddharth walk into the office along with Mona, both looking stunned and mesmerised. Apparently, Siddh had volunteered to drop Mona home as it was on the way to his house in Navi Mumbai, but had to make a hasty retreat due to the heavy water logging. An incident they shared was heart wrenching. They were very upset as they had seen a man walk his way to death into an invisible manhole. It is one thing to live a harsh life, but it is cruel to witness death as a process from such close quarters. Mona couldn't hold herself any longer. I saw her rushing to the cafeteria. I instinctively followed her. She sat down and started sobbing. I put my arm around her and sympathetically asked her what had happened. "That man was somebody's husband, son, father, brother Sri, but he was gone in a matter of a few seconds. We just couldn't do anything. He simply drowned," and broke into uncontrollable sobs. I fetched her a glass of water to calm her down.

Meanwhile, the entire office along with Siddh had assembled at the cafeteria. The horror stories were flying in thick and fast. Somebody had got swept away by the rains, some people had got electrocuted in different places in Mumbai city, and so on and so forth. Luckily, the office TV was able to relay live news about the water attack that had struck the city, but there was no guarantee the cable connection would last for long. We all were in a similar predicament, none of us knew the status of our family members and our family had no clue about us. Siddh had a good presence of mind and quickly instructed the cafeteria staff to prepare as much food as possible and store as much drinking water as possible, as all of us were going to be stuck in the office the whole night. He also instructed the house keeping staff to store as much water as possible in the washrooms as water and electricity supply too would soon get cut.

Night dawned, but the rains only seemed to increase in ferocity. Water, cable and electricity succumbed to the torrent. We all found our places in the office/cafeteria to lie down and sleep in a bid to momentarily forget the horror that had struck the city, the heaviest downpour in decades. Mona still looked stunned and found herself a chair to rest on. I sat beside her and lightly kept stroking her hair to comfort her. What struck me was I was more concerned about her well being than not being able to inform my family about my safety, or check about their predicament. Mona too seemed more concerned about the family which had lost its beloved to a treacherous manhole than not being able to inform her family about her own predicament or find out whether her father had reached home safely from work. It was not that we were not concerned about our families. We all found ourselves in a common predicament. We drew moral solace from one another, as none of us was able to reach out to our family members. Even those who stayed relatively close to the office were unable to get home. Twenty of us, including some of our agents, were hauled up in that dark room, only slightly brightened by a couple of candles.

As the night dragged along – it indeed was the longest night of our lives – as life insurance professionals we realised this was a moment of truth for us. We kept talking to one another about how life insurance was not just about fulfilling targets, rather it was about insuring people. Our conscience bit us as we recalled with frankness the number of times we had pushed a sale just to please our Boss, or to meet our elusive targets. Mona however was quiet and seemed half as sleep. I became concerned and tried being close to her. I tried talking to her so that she remained alert, helped her eat some food and have some water.

As the night kept getting longer and a few of my colleagues sauntered into sleep, I stayed close to Mona. As the candle light slightly lit up her face, I noticed her sharp features and stylish hairstyle. For the first time I saw her at such close quarters and felt like planting a light kiss on her forehead. I began to understand that my feelings for her at that point were not just one of sympathy. There was more to it than that. As I battled between my emotions for Mona and the eerie atmosphere of the night, with sounds of the lashing rain still prominently striking my ears, I realised I was in love, not only with Mona, but also with my parents and my brother, as I deeply started missing them. I became extremely concerned about them and had tears in my eyes. Just as I had tried to give comfort to Mona, I wished she would get up, hug me and caress my head with her warm palms. She looked extremely loving to me that night, but I had to manage my emotions and the pain of sitting through a wet horror story.

I kept reflecting on the amount of panic and chaos that would have been unleashed on the city. I wondered how many would have died, and also how many carried enough insurance on their head. I mentally calculated my own portfolio and realised I had a major marking-up to do. The night wore on and I finally fell asleep due to sheer mental and emotional exhaustion.

Around 6 am a buzz around the office woke me up. The few, who had got up, were seen waking others up. They were updating that the rains had subsided substantially, and that we should try to make our way home slowly and carefully. I saw Mona had also woken up and was heading towards me. "Sri, why don't you join me with Boss in the car? We'll drop you somewhere," she said. "Yes," I replied in a half-sleepy state.

Soon we all headed towards the basement to check out one another's cars, but realised there was no basement in sight. How can a basement get washed away, we wondered! But then the horror struck us: all the cars lay submerged under the water. For the first time I saw Siddh get emotional and very upset. With light sobs, he said he had bought the luxury car just a month back. Bosses normally try to hold their emotions back so that they don't appear weak, but at that moment Siddh had cracked, perhaps also as a culmination of the stress he was experiencing since the previous evening. As the branch head, the responsibility of our safety was on him. "Be strong Boss. Everything's going to be fine," Mona tried assuring him. A few other colleagues' cars also lay submerged and they were downcast. The water logging in and around the building too had not receded enough for any of us to move out.

So we all were back in office, wondering what to do next. In the next half hour or so, the rains completely stopped. This was a huge relief, which meant in some time the water would recede and each one of us could head home. In a while, somebody's mobile rang and we looked in that direction. It was Mona's. We simultaneously checked our networks and immediately tried reaching out to our family members. "I am fine," Mona said very emotionally. Her father had called. The signals had got revived, but none of our phones were yet active. I wondered whether the service provider had also fallen in love with her. Everybody in her house was safe. Soon enough, we all were using her phone to inform and check on our people. But a few of us, including me, could not connect as our family members' mobile and landline connections were not active as yet.

At around 10 am, we all left office to go home as the rains had stopped, the sun had slightly come out and the water had receded. Each male member took responsibility to drop their female colleagues home, that is, whoever lived in proximity. For others, we managed to tag them with friends in other offices in the same building. Siddh decided to drop Mona home and I took upon myself the responsibility of a couple of my female colleagues. As we all prepared to disburse, Mona and I hugged each other. "Try calling me once you get home," I said. "You too," she said, as both of our eyes stayed locked for a while. I could see a sense of gratitude in her eyes and I wondered what she spotted in my eyes.

It was an arduous journey back home. Bus stops and railways stations were jam packed. My mobile got discharged and so anyway could not call home. I was worried about my family members. We had to walk quite a bit through water logged areas, very careful that we did not run into an open manhole. We tried holding each other's hands as we waded through shin deep water. Through a combination of walking, train and bus, after dropping my female colleagues home, I finally managed to reach home at 7 pm.

As I prepared to enter my house, I found the door ajar and could hear sob sounds of my mother, who was surrounded by our neighbours. As soon as I entered the house, my mother let out a huge cry and rushed to hug me. My father and brother, who were sitting crestfallen in one corner, also rushed towards me. I could sense that they had lost hope of seeing me. On TV, most horror stories were being relayed from areas near my office. I too was thrilled to be home with my family and cried my heart out. Even I had to hold my tears for many hours since the last evening. The horror had lasted over 24 hours. As a unit, we never felt closer to each other – it was as if Mom, Dad, Krish and me were experiencing new-found love. It is moments such as these that bring out the richness of emotions we have for each other. Thankfully, my father and brother did not have to undergo any ordeal. My brother had come back early from work as he was feeling a little unwell, and my father had taken a day off from work, which I was not aware of as I had left home early.

I profusely thanked all my neighbours for being with my family and enquired about their family members' well being. Thankfully, there was no bad news from any of the 30 flats that comprised our society. That day brought to my light the value of living in a co-operative society, where, while there are differences, occasions such as these unite people across caste and religion like never before. After all, humanity is the biggest religion, isn't it?

As I prepared to freshen up and have something to eat, I quickly hooked my mobile to the charger so that I could enquire about Mona's well being. Her expression when we left office was still fresh in my mind. I wondered at what time she would have reached home. The mobile had been discharged for quite sometime and so it took a while for it come on, adding to my anxiety. The landline still lay dead. But soon enough I heard a message tone on my mobile, in fact a few message tones. One of them was Mona's. "Hi Sri, reached home safe. Boss was fantastically caring. Hope you reached safely too." I immediately dialed her number and was delighted to hear her voice - a barrage of questions greeted me. "Hi Sri. Where are you? How are you? You are fine?" Mona was extremely concerned. "Hey sweetheart (don't know how that came out and she didn't mind it either), I am fine. Good to hear your voice." "Same here. Thanks a lot for your support. You really took care of me yesterday. Will never forget that." "Wasn't I just doing my duty?," I asked. "Sure, but a friend in need is a friend indeed." I could now sense the warmth from across the phone too. On that rainy evening and night, something between us had definitely changed, forever.

Mumbai remained shut for a couple of days. The newspapers and television channels were full of heart-wrenching stories of how some people, in a bid to save their car, had died in it as their power windows had stopped functioning and the water had entered the car, of how some people had slipped into a manhole and also of how some people had got electrocuted. But there were also some great humane stories, truly reflecting the spirit of Mumbai. People had invited home strangers stuck in the rain and gave them food, shelter and clothing till they were able to get back to their locations. Few auto rickshaw and cab drivers braved gushing waters to drive home young girls and women. No wonder, Mumbai as a city is said to be the safest for women.

Any other city would have taken at least a month to resemble normalcy. But Mumbai was on its feet, and up and running in less than 72 hours. Attendance in offices had touched 80 per cent within three days of the rains, and Mona and I were part of the 'spirited people of Mumbai' who got back to work sooner than later. Our colleagues' cars came out after the water had receded. Luckily, the damage was minimal and all of them started driving them back to work in quick time. My Boss was of course relieved, both with the fact that his car was in good condition, and also that his staff and agents were safe. Fortunately, our company also reported that all its employees and agents in its Mumbai offices were safe.

We were reunited after three 'long' days, and occupied our seats as usual at the cafeteria, relieved that life was limping back to normal in Mumbai. They say human memory is short, but Mumbai uses this phenomenon to its advantage. Mumbaiites quickly put tragedies behind them and move on – maybe because of the exciting pace of the city, maybe the daily struggle is always bigger than the biggest of tragedies, maybe that is in the genes of the Mumbai masses. We discussed this and a few other aspects of Mumbai and also the emotional 'reunion' with our respective families. We both realised the need to spend more time with our respective families, and also how much they meant to us.

I will never forget the hug my parents and brother gave me on returning home. It just showed how much I mattered to them. Close relationships are something we take for granted, but moments such as these bring alive the emotional fabric of our lives. Just imagine how life would be if our family was not around for us.

Mona too had had an emotional reunion. She said when she reached near her home, there were so many people shedding tears of joy that it seemed the entire colony was present to see her alive and well. She said she had to hug a few people before presenting herself in front of her parents and sister. They simply jumped on her and hugged her so tightly as if to say they would never ever let her go off from them again. Her father, after an arduous journey, had managed to come home by midnight. That day, both of us acknowledged that we felt closer to our respective families, but stopped shy of expressing the greater closeness between us.

I realised I was in love and I could sense that Mona too had a twinkle in her eyes whenever she saw me. But I resisted making any further moves as it was time to re-focus on work, as a sales manager's job involved constant pressure of recruitment and sales.

Love anyway cannot be a full time profession for people in sales. Mona and I however did start spending a lot more of our 'spare' time together. Our chatting camp had unconsciously stretched itself to beyond the boundaries of the cafeteria to roadside tea stalls, Udipi restaurants and coffee joints. We both realised – without saying it of course – that we enjoyed each other's company more and more, and also we missed each other's company more and more.

In my lonely moments I reflected upon how love had two sides – the joy of meeting and the pain of missing (God only knows how I became a sales guy, when I should have actually become a professor of philosophy or literature. Strange are the ways of God!). Soon enough, we were watching movies together and meeting over weekends for dinner. Of course, by now we were each other's best friends.

They say love makes the world go around. In my case, love had created a turnaround. There was more energy in what I did. I felt more happy from inside. All this reflected in my job performance. In a matter of months, I was the No 2 performer in my branch, and in the Top 10 all Mumbai, and was due for a promotion. There was a spring in my steps and I had become bold enough to shower Mona with small gifts from time to time, like perfumes, purses, etc. She wasn't too far behind either. She too gifted me a watch, a wallet and an out-of-fashion walkman. Interestingly, all four words: watch, wallet, walkman and woman begin with the alphabet W, and by extension even wife. Of course, in our respective homes they thought we were on some senseless buying spree.

Soon enough, it became clear that I would be promoted to Assistant Branch Manager (ABM) position. When I broke the news to my family, my mother prepared special *payasam* (sweet made from rice and milk), and got busy informing our relatives about my promotion. I suspect she simply grabbed the opportunity to 'hit back' at some relatives who had subtly enquired about her sons' career progress, or the lack of it, and openly expressed about their wards' growth.

Many of my cousins were abroad, earning dollar salaries, having settled there after MS or MBA, or CA, or CS, etc. The MSes and MBAs were in the US and the CAs and CSes were in Dubai and Abu Dhabi. The increment after promotion would perhaps not even fund their weekend holiday expenses. But my mother was excited and I was happy I had given her a reason to be so. And anyway making a larger-than-life case about promotions is part of Indian service class culture – after all, is that not the purpose of life – getting promotions? She felt sad about one thing though. "I wish your brother had already got married. I could have found a nice girl for you also," she said. "Damn it," I told myself, "problem of chronology again."

But that statement also made me realise how important timing of a marriage proposal is for Indians when it comes to arranged marriages. You are likely to get a 'better' girl if you have recently got a promotion. As in sales, closing as a technique is very important in the marriage market too. But what they don't budget for is job promotions are likely to continue post marriage too, but you cannot ask for a 'better' wife then, can you?

After marriage your performance and capability are measured by how quickly you gift a grandchild to your parents and how quickly you follow up with another one. If a third one arrives too, then your relatives suspect that besides sleeping with your wife there is little else you do in life.

Horoscopes play an important part in a traditional TamBrahm Iyer marriage process. If the horoscopes don't match, it is quits anyway. In many cases, the horoscope comes first and other details follow only if the stars have an alignment. Seen from this perspective, in an arranged marriage, love between a Tamil husband and his wife is a function of many things matching and few mismatches which cannot be matched. But surely, at least hopefully, two people who live together long enough do grow fond of each other – and perhaps that explains the success of arranged marriages in our country despite two strangers agreeing to spend the rest of their lives together. The secret lies in the great Indian tradition of tolerance. Comparatively, love marriages are yet to match up to the credibility and longevity of arranged marriages.

Mona too was very happy for me. We eagerly awaited my promotion letter and thereafter a formal announcement. An ABM's role also meant an opportunity to hone my leadership skills, as it involved a few junior managers reporting to me. I looked forward to that assignment as it was exciting to teach and coach your team, and in Siddh I had a Boss who was adept at people management skills.

There had developed between Mona and me a chemistry which resulted in often both of us guessing right what we were thinking. We had now started putting our arms around each other in public and holding hands and walking, even though neither of us had said "I Love You" so far. It came naturally to us and there was no awkwardness. But I felt there was a need for a formal sealing of the relationship. I for sure wanted to spend the rest of my life with her. It was not that I was madly in love and couldn't live without her, but I knew I wanted her to be with me all my life. And if marriage was an inevitability, then it was Mona whom I wanted to marry.

Soon enough, my promotion was announced and I had to throw a party for my colleagues whose primary interest was to have some booze at my expense. I kept my lady colleagues out of it, as I did not trust my male friends' behaviours after being two pegs down. My lady colleagues were quite happy with some sweets. As for Mona, I had a different plan. I decided to take her to a lavish restaurant over the weekend for dinner and propose to her there.

The day was fixed for Saturday at one of South Mumbai's posh restaurants. I had a table reserved for just the two of us. I waited for Mona at the hotel lobby, dressed in a brand new purple half shirt and black trouser. She arrived on time wearing a wonderful pink salwar kameez with matching bindi and sandals. Her short hair was combed with care and sat elegantly on her intelligent head. Wonderful gold ear rings hung with grace. She looked beautiful and I felt like planting a kiss on her broad forehead. We hadn't yet moved beyond holding of hands, or putting our arms on each other's shoulders. Therefore, a kiss at that point would have been like crossing the Wagah border. Also, we Tamils are trained to hold hands and kiss only after marriage. I had already violated one rule, going beyond that would have meant discarding all cultural virtues I had been brought up with. So more from a perspective of preserving whatever values was left than anything else, I decided to refrain from kissing her forehead, which unlike kissing on the lips, is actually a safe bet in modern boy-girl relationships. Instead, I paid her a compliment. "You look stunning," I said. Mona smiled from ear to ear at the compliment, and then we both moved towards our reserved table.

Dinner was wonderful. I ordered her favourite dishes and we chatted like long-lost friends. We even danced to the wonderful live soft music being doled out, with arms around each other's back – the lines were beginning to get crossed. The wonderful evening was coming to an end. As we were about to leave, Mona pulled out something from a bag which she had placed carefully next to her seat. It was a gift for me – in fact a couple of them, a lovely red colour tie and an expensive watch. "This is for you Sri, my best friend," she said with great feeling and warmth, and handed it over to me. I was touched by her gesture and instantly felt the timing was perfect for the planned proposal. I had planned to propose to her as we walked along Marine Drive post dinner, as the mammoth Arabian Sea could serve as a perfect backdrop for life's mammoth question: Will you marry me? But I felt God had provided just the perfect setting for a perfect end to a perfect evening.

I sat up straight, looked at the gifts, then at Mona, and said: "I will take the gifts with me only if you agree to something." "What?" "Will you marry me sweetheart? I love you and want to spend the rest of my life with you," I said with as much emotion as I could summon. Immediately, Mona got up from her seat and started moving towards me. It surprised me, but there was nothing in her facial expression that suggested she was angry or upset. As she came near, I got up and we stood face to face for a few moments that seemed like ages to me. Then she hugged me lightly and said: "Of course I will *Mr Buddhu* (means silly person in Hindi)," and started laughing so loudly that the whole restaurant could hear her laughter. I was stunned by the matter-of-fact way in which she had responded to what I assumed would be an Earth-shaking or Earth-shattering – depending on which way it goes – moment in life. "Can we leave now my to-be hubby?," she asked, more as a command than as a question, and dragged me out of there. In that excitement, we both forgot to settle the bill. So that had the waiter running after us. I apologised and paid the bill.

Soon we were sitting on the parapet which acts as a boundary for the sea. With our fingers locked into each other's, we sat silently for a while, listening to the sound of the waves behind us. I sensed that something dramatically had altered in our lives, but Mona had made it look so simple. She had once again demonstrated her elegance and confidence. Mona broke the ice. She moved her face closer to mine, held my cheeks lightly with her right hand and said: "I love you too Sri. What made you take so long to say this? If you had not said it today, I would have in a few days time," she said with an emotion which was as genuine as the bright light of the moon, which was right above us, as if to communicate that this alliance had divine permission. I looked intently into her eyes for a while, slowly removed her right palm from my cheek and kissed it – thereby breaking the next cultural virtue too. She immediately hugged me tightly, unconscious of the people taking a walk along the footpath, watching us. We stayed in each other's arms for quite some time, eyes closed, basking in the moments that would forever remain etched in our memories.

We had travelled a whole journey – from comfort to liking, to deep friendship to love, and now to commitment. I think it is beautiful to love, but it is hard to commit, that's why maybe many lovers take a while before they are ready to marry each other. Love brings two people closer, but marriage takes away a piece of each other to create a new 'US', and this transition from YOU to US is perhaps the most defining moment in any individual's life, and on that moonlit night, we had decided to make the transition. We both were in deep reverie, and it took a phone call from her mother to break the train of emotions and thoughts. It was already 11 pm and so we rushed in a cab to drop her home. Of course, I just saw her off at her colony's gate and proceeded towards my home, which was a good half an hour away at least.

That night I lay on bed reflecting long on my relationship with Mona and the way ahead. That night I felt happy, contented and fulfilled. My whole frame was reveling in the soft touch of Mona, which I consciously tried to hold on to. The elixir of a woman's touch who so intensely loved you was a totally new experience for me. If the phone had not rung, maybe we would have been locked in each other's arms the whole night. I wondered why holding a woman's hand was taboo before marriage. After all, it simply transported you to a different world. But the adult in me reasoned that the values our parents gave us were right; after all, a man-woman relationship is the most delicate one and the thin line of difference between lust and love is not realised often, leading to various immoral and anti-social behaviours. At one level, my heart was at its happiest, and at another, my mind was reasoning, rationalising and questioning. I asked myself whether I felt guilty about getting physical with Mona. My mind was unsure, but my heart was clear.

As I continued to grapple with some more thoughts, sleep took over and brought to an end a day when I had decided to permanently give away a piece of myself to the woman I loved – Mona.

MASALA PAPAD

Drama-Cum-Melodrama

A month had passed since that Sunday when we had dropped a bombshell on our parents. Mona's parents were pressurising her to quit her job, stay home and go through the arranged marriage process. The middle lady who arranges marriages had become a frequent visitor. Her mother had got in touch with some Baba to do some special pujas so that Mona could regain her 'sense of judgement'. Sindhis, unlike Tamilians, while fixing arranged marriages, lay less emphasis on horoscopes and more on family background, financial well being, character, and enquiries about the family. Not that Tamil families do not lay emphasis on all these aspects, but the main protagonist in their case is the horoscope.

Sindhi families normally meet either in hotels or temple compounds, where a few of their family members watch the prospective bride and bridegroom from a distance and form an opinion based upon height, weight, appearance, etc. Both the boy and girl spend some time together to understand whether they can strike it off with each other for life. Of course, some families go home visiting too. It all depends upon how the middle lady plays her cards. It is a big time business for these ladies and they get a fat pie from both sides. Mona hated every bit of this process and tried resisting complying with her family with all her might. She was also everyday surrounded by 'counselors' in the form of elderly relatives, of course summoned by her mother.

Tensions between her and her parents had reached very uncomfortable proportions.

Mona increasingly seemed unhappy and it pained me that I was the cause for it. Since the time we had said yes to each other, I had started loving her even more and started feeling increasingly insecure about losing her. At my place, my parents avoided discussion and, instead, started putting pressure on my brother to get married fast, so that they could look for a good Tamil alliance for me too. They felt I had had a 'Sindhi digression' only because my brother was not clearing the tracks for me. I once overheard my parents talking, "Sri has fallen into bad ways due to our irresponsible Krish."

Many people in this world as a habit cannot keep anything in their stomach, and my mother is one of them. She publicised about my 'wrong ways' and I too had some elderly relatives calling me and advising me on how I should not fall into the trap of Sindhis, for whom culture means nothing and only money means everything.

Some of them even suggested that Sindhi girls have many boy friends before getting married. "Sri you should not trouble your parents in their old age. And also you must wait for your brother to get married. You have no respect for your elder brother also? Don't worry, we will find you a suitable Tamil girl very soon after your brother gets married," one uncle said, absolutely trying my patience.

Everyday my house was full of stories about how inter-caste and love marriages do not work. It was about how western influence had spoilt our culture. My father even went to the extent of suggesting Sindhis are foreigners as they came from Pakistan and do not even have a state of their own.

I felt irritated that Mona and me had become public knowledge. My brother too shouted at my parents, especially my mother, as to why she was going around publicising the whole issue. It was an internal family matter and should be kept that way, he said. To this, my mother with tears in her eyes responded: "Now you also support him. Go, you also go and find a Punjabi for yourself, and me and your father will learn to eat paneer, chicken, egg and mutton." We brothers wondered whether food was the real issue. We found it amusing and angering at the same time.

The whole episode brought Krish and me closer. "Sri, you go ahead and get married. I will stand by you. I am in no hurry to get married. I will marry only when I want to and nobody can blackmail me into it," he said. My parents refused to even meet Mona, but I arranged for a meeting between Mona and my brother. Krish found her pretty and sensible, and after meeting her, he more vociferously started supporting my decision to marry her. "Right choice Bro," he said. Mona's parents too steadfastly refused to meet me.

But the hullabaloos at our respective places started taking a toll on our equanimity. By now our colleagues had got a wind of what was happening in our lives. My Boss kept a close watch on my performance, as at no cost, he said, he wanted my personal matters to affect mine and the office's performance. But I realised it was only a matter of time before my performance took a hit. The situation had started to get out of control, and so in a fit of rage – or inspiration – I decided to declare *Halla Bol* (literally, raise your voice, and in this context, kind of mini war) on mine and Mona's parents. It is funny how the very people whom you felt so close to and indebted to post the rain havoc in the city had turned villains now. The very people without whom we felt life would not be worth it just sometime back were now the biggest pain in our lives. The very people who had fed us, brought us up and prayed for us had now become the greatest stumbling block.

One evening, as both of us sat in an Udipi restaurant, I shared my intention with Mona. "Let's run away. We both are financially independent. Let us declare Halla Bol," I said, both with intent as well as frustration in my voice. Mona was silent for a while. She then looked at me intently and said: "No Sri. We are not doing that. We will either get married with our parents' blessings or we will not get married." I was stunned and felt let down. I felt I was ready to sacrifice my family for her, but she was not ready to leave hers for me. I wondered if she really loved me. "But I promise you Sri, if I can't get married to you, I will never get married in my life," she said with tears in her eyes. I felt very small in front of her now after all those thoughts that had crossed my mind just a while back. "Me too dear," I said and tightly held both her hands, buried my head into them and started to sob. Luckily, there was nobody else in the AC section of the hotel, and, therefore, both of us could give vent to our feelings. Mona slowly caressed my hair and provided me with a much-needed motherly touch. Who said women become a mother only after marriage? They are born mothers. But unfortunately, like Mona's and my mother, many of them lose perspective the moment their children make independent choices, especially regarding their marriage.

Things dragged along for some more time. Both of us realised we needed a break from work, as balancing emotions at home and professionalism at work was taking its toll on both of us. So we both went to Siddh and asked for leave for 15 days, which he readily granted, both out of sympathy as well as out of adherence to HR rules. The rules disallowed leave being denied if it was pending, and in any case we were not from the same department. Both Mona and me decided to use these 15 days to try and convince our parents to at least meet each other once. The one thing going for us was my brother's support.

Mona swung into action at her place, and we brothers got together at my place. "I wish to marry Mona only if you are ready for it. We could have run away and nobody could have stopped us. But what is the use of marrying that way? If you bless us, great; if not, I will take a transfer out of Mumbai and never get married. Mona too will plan to leave the city. Please don't think this is some filmi comment," I told my parents with great intent, with my brother alongside. My parents got a shock of their life. They had not expected me to confront them in this way. This was a different kind of *satyagraha*. But they still stoically held on to their position, and there followed a long silence. For the next few days, there was no conversation between me and my parents.

Mona too had planned to use the same script. We had done some rehearsals to get the emotion, tone and mood right. In sales, we are used to using scripts to 'trap' our prospects. While we meant every word of what we said, we just put a process to it. It hadn't worked for me. I wondered how it was shaping up at Mona's place.

Mona's words actually stunned her parents. Her mother started sobbing, feeling remorseful at her daughter's words. Her father, who had not expected such strong emotions from his daughter, went into deep silence with his head bowed down. He felt let down and hurt. But he chose not to respond, and after some time, simply got up and locked himself inside his room. Pinky, witnessing all this drama, felt terrified, and sat next to Mona clutching her hands tightly.

Our 15 days of leave finally came to an end and both Mona and I met one evening at one of the coffee shops to decide on the further course of action. Both of us found it extremely difficult to concentrate on our work. We also could not bear to see each other's worn-down faces, which looked as if the whole world had ganged up against us. I began to feel that the emotions shown in Hindi films in such situations were actually a mirror image of what happened in reality, the only difference being we could not break into a sad song.

Though we had stepped into the coffee shop to discuss, we simply could not converse. Two grief-stricken souls had assembled at a coffee joint where we saw many couples holding hands and muttering sweet nothings into each other's ears, and here we were, communicating sorrow and nothing else. I finally took a deep breath and decided to break the uncomfortable silence. "So, what do we do now?" "I am resigning tomorrow. A friend of mine has forwarded my resume to a company in Nagpur and they are interested in hiring me. The formal interview is yet to happen, but I can't work here anymore," Mona said. I was stunned. The only motivation for me to come to office was I could get to meet Mona. "Ok, in that case, I will resign too." "No, please don't do that Sri. I understand your feelings, but don't do that. Find another job first and then resign," Mona said, expressing herself in a very concerned tone. I simply stayed silent. We ordered coffee, drank it in silence, and left for our respective homes feeling sad and demoralised.

Mona resigned the next day. I took a day off and went to watch a movie all alone, simply to change my mood. Of course, nobody in my family, including my brother knew I was not attending office on that day. Post that, a few days passed with me contemplating my next professional move, as I could no longer work in the office where Mona was not there. She told Siddh she could not serve the 30 days notice period due to the extraordinary situation at her home. He understood and accordingly arranged with HR for her speedy release from the job.

Mona and I kept in touch on phone, but the joy and words had gone out of our lives. The interactions became less. We were not on talking terms with our parents. Life had become a burden and love the single biggest problem creator. Our self respect had taken a severe beating. As adults we hated being told what to do with our lives. If not for Mona's firm stand that running away and getting married was not an option, I was all set for a filmi-style wedding. We both had enough sympathetic friends who would have supported us. I thought of broaching the subject with Mona again, but could not muster the courage to do so, as I somewhere respected her value system and did not want to risk upsetting her further.

A month had passed since Mona had left. My job performance started dropping. My Boss tried his best to be patient with me, but obviously, beyond a point he could not be understanding. He called me to his cabin and put forward a proposal: "Sri, I know what you are going through. I think you need a change of location. Would you like to take a transfer to the Pune office? They are looking for somebody with your caliber." I accepted immediately. Things moved fast and within a week I had a formal letter of transfer in hand. I had to report to Pune within the next seven days. By now, Mona also closed her negotiations with the company in Nagpur. They wanted her to join immediately. It was now time to drop another bombshell at our respective homes.

It was weeks since a normal conversation had taken place between me and my parents. My brother too was busy with his work, and though sympathetic towards my cause, could not give me much time. On the day I received the transfer letter, I decided to break the news to my family soon after dinner. *"Amma, Appa,* I know you don't want to talk to me, but I have some news for you. You won't have to suffer me anymore, as I am taking a transfer to Pune and have to report there next week." "What?," my brother reacted. My parents, who all these days had been behaving as if I was the single biggest mistake of their lives, had a wake-up call. They realised that

I meant every word of what I had said. The prospect of me not marrying anybody else too and staying away from home seemed real.

My mother, with whom I did not have eye contact for weeks, started sobbing. After her tears had subsided, she cleared her throat to say something. But my father, sensing that this was an extraordinary situation, stopped her from saying anything, and spoke instead. "Sri, we are not your enemies. Don't give us such pain in our old age. Don't go anywhere because of us. We only feel that this alliance is not good for you. But if you feel so strongly about it, we have no objection. It is your life. Anyway, these days where do children listen to their parents? But your in-laws must come and see us and discuss the formalities."

"What are you saying?," my mother asked, breaking into loud sobs. But my father took her in his arms and consoled her. "Let us not stretch this matter any further. It is his life. He alone is responsible if anything goes wrong," he told my mother, both with a sense of resignation, as well as practicality. Krish and me looked at each other with a sense of relief. "Thanks *Appa*. I assure you Mona is a great girl. Krish has met her. You both will also like her. But it is subject to her parents also agreeing to the alliance," I said. I sincerely hoped Mona's parents would also change their attitude once their daughter told them that she was shifting to Nagpur.

I called up Mona and narrated to her the whole turn of events. There was excitement in my voice. But her voice hardly communicated any sense of optimism. "Sorry Sri. It is too late now. I told them about Nagpur and they said they will not bow down to such blackmailing tactics. They said they will neither let me go to Nagpur nor let me get married to you." With my optimism having receded as quickly as it had surfaced, I asked her in a voice epitomising disappointment, "What will you do now dear?" "I don't know," she said, and sobbing, kept the phone down.

I informed my brother and parents about Mona's predicament. Krish felt sorry for both of us. My parents tried their best to hide their happiness at the turn of events in their favour, and that too in a matter of minutes of my father agreeing to our relationship. But I somehow felt my father was not entirely happy. He seemed concerned about how I was going to cope with all this.

As my departure date for Pune closed in, I was shattered and in no mood to go to Pune either. My hopes had risen and fallen as fast as a giant wheel goes up and comes down. My colleagues had planned a farewell for me on my last day in the Mumbai office. I was in no mood for any celebrations and farewell speeches. I was also very concerned about Mona. She had withdrawn into a shell. We kept in touch through phone. There was a cold war at her home and she didn't have the heart to 'run away' to Nagpur, as she felt that would complicate matters further. She felt let down.

As for me, I decided not to turn up at office on my farewell day. Instead, I emailed my resignation to Siddh, as I felt, because of my personal problems I had no business to be disengaged from my work. I took Krish into confidence before resigning and informed my parents accordingly. Siddh tried to speak to me, but I did not take his calls. He messaged: "Sri, I am not accepting your resignation. When you feel better, come and meet me. We will discuss."

I started admiring the human side of my Boss. He was a task master, but now I understood why despite his ruthless streak for numbers, people hardly left him. He had one of the lowest team attritions pan India.

My parents tried to reason with me that I should not leave a job because of a girl, and that too a Sindhi. "Sri, this is not a Hindi film. This is life," my father told me sternly. For a middle class TamBrahm Iyer service class family, nothing is more disastrous than somebody quitting his job. Values of loyalty and hard work are embedded into our psyche from childhood. My father and many people of his generation had dedicated their whole life to an organisation. Their moment of nirvana was the twenty five years of service medal, the provident fund and gratuity that would come at the end of a long journey of a job that had provided them and their family with so much security. Resigning from a job is not something that even crossed their minds. For them, me leaving my job was a greater sin than loving a non-vegetarian-eating Sindhi girl.

My mother was about to get into one of her melodramatic moods. She lamented: "What will we tell our relatives? What is our future? What will happen to Sri? Sensing that she was getting herself into dangerous zones, Krish blurted out: "You are concerned about our relatives who are only interested in gossiping? I don't care what they have to say. We all have to be happy and Sri has to get his peace of mind back. That's all I am interested in. And in any case, what's the big deal about a job? Sri will get another one."

Obviously, we brothers came from vastly different schools of thought as compared to our parents. I felt by resigning I had actually shown great loyalty to my organisation, as I was not prepared to selfishly draw a salary and not put in my best. If I could not do my best for my company which gave me financial sustenance, I better get out. To my mind, that was a great value system to practice. Krish understood and respected my decision.

As the days passed, life was sober but highly uninteresting at my place. I fluctuated between brooding and telling myself that this is not the end of the world. Actually, I felt guilty about landing Mona in such a big mess. I told her to accept things as they were and move on in life. I told her to do as her parents said and get back to a job. "Let us honour our decision not to go against them. We will always remain friends. I want you to be happy. For my sake, restore normalcy to your life," I told her. "Yes Sri. I will try. But you also promise me that you will go back to your job in the same office, or find another one quickly." "I promise."

I found the latter option better, joining some other company. At least that will help me get away from a context and help build my life afresh. We kind of accepted our predicament as God's will and tried to move on. The pain of the situation was becoming unbearable for us. We could always live with good memories about each other, if not with each other, we reasoned. I went to meet Siddh finally and asked him for one last favour – to place me in another company. Incredibly, he did it with just a phone call to a friend, and I had my offer letter in hand within three days.

Mona too started looking for a job. Siddh asked her to join back, but she refused. Somewhere, Mona was more consumed by the situation than I was. She was a lady with a lot of positive pride. She was confident and liked to lead life on her own terms. Though she did not want to go against her parents, she was hurt by their reaction and all the drama they had created around this whole episode. She decided she was going to do something about it. Something inside her told her that our relationship had not ended – not yet.

So one Sunday she called for a 'formal' meeting between her and her parents. She decided to bring into force all the tactics that go into handling difficult customers, and her parents were just that – difficult customers. She decided to confront and communicate, rather than just confront, as was more or less the case so far. After a quiet lunch, at the appointed hour, the three adults in the family met at the living room. Mona had packed Pinky off to her friend's house.

"Papa, Mamma," Mona began, "I am sorry if I have hurt you in any way in the last few weeks. But don't you think I have the right to decide about my future and who I want to spend the rest of my life with? I am your daughter. You have given me the best of values. Do you think I will ever do anything wrong or irresponsible?" There was silence for a while, then her mother started sobbing, and said: "You have already done something irresponsible by loving that Madrasi." "His name is Srikkanth," an irritated Mona responded. Her father, normally a person with a quiet demeanour, too got irritated with his sobbing wife. "Ro na munjhi maa. Monaji gaal tha budh." (Don't cry my mother. At least listen to what Mona has to say). "Chou putta," (say son) he told Mona reassuringly (*Sindhis generally refer to their children as putta, which literally means son*).

"Thanks Papa." Looking straight into his eyes, Mona asked her father the game-changing question: "Do you trust me Papa?" Another uncomfortable silence ensued. Within this simple question lies the moment of truth for parents. If they say no, it reflects more on their upbringing than on their children's character. "Yes Mona, we trust you....but....." "But what Papa?" "We are concerned about how you will adjust in a different culture. We don't even have any South Indian friend. I have heard South Indians are very conservative and we have brought you up with so much freedom. I don't think you will be happy. If you marry somebody from our community, we will not have to worry. Mirchandani's son is also a nice boy. They are like us."

Mona was wearing her customer-centricity hat, but the mention of her father's friend's son almost transformed her into a rebel again. But she simply bit her tongue, controlled herself and continued to speak with composure. "I understand Papa, but even if Sri was not there in my life, I would have never agreed to marry his son. I don't like him. And in any case what is the guarantee that all people who get married within their community are happy? Remember Raju's marriage? Both the families knew each other very well, but what happened? They landed in court. In contrast, you see Praveen. He married a Gujarati girl and for the last so many years they are so happy. She has adapted to our culture. I will also learn Sri's culture."

This set her father thinking. He loved his daughter more than he hated her marrying a non-Sindhi. The events of the last few weeks had deeply affected him too. He had secretly explored with his friends examples of people who had chosen inter-caste marriages. His own data was not as bad as his own feelings about Mona's choice, and Mona too now presented certain facts he could not refute. He also understood that times had changed, and children made their own decisions. Somewhere, he was afraid of antagonising her too much, as that might have serious repercussions. In Indian society, a girl's father carries many unexpressed fears, and ultimately, often chooses discretion over valour. Deep within, he also appreciated Mona's decision not to walk out on her parents, which as a financially independent professional she could have done.

After a prolonged silence and some more sobs from her mother, Mr Manohar Punjabi spoke again: "Ok *beta* (*which literally means son in Hindi*), if you have already decided to marry him only, so be it. But there is only one request. I would like to take an opinion from Anand uncle. If he clears him I have no objection. But it is only a request. If you feel there is no need for that, call him next Sunday for lunch," he said with a sense of resignation. "But what will we tell our relatives?," her mother interrupted. "We'll handle that. It's her life, not theirs," her father said, displaying a maturity befitting the 21st century.

Mr Anand Bhatia was a relative and friend of Mona's father. He was one of those Sindhis who had stayed away from the family business and built his career in the corporate world. An engineer by profession, he had grown up in Salem in the South and therefore could speak fluent Tamil. Mona's father wanted him to take my 'interview', as he felt being a service person and somebody who was aware of the Tamil language and culture, Mr Anand could ask me the right questions. Mona did not like the idea as she knew Mr Anand could be a bit curt, and a sensitive person like me may feel hurt. But she didn't want to upset her father any further, and so decided to ask me if I would oblige. "I will also accompany you," she assured. "Will you please do this for me Sri?" "Sure."

After Mona had narrated the whole conversation with her parents, I was convinced she belonged to the sales profession. She disarmed her opponents not through confrontation, but by asking the right questions and presenting relevant data. She could teach a thing or two about handling customers to chatty salespeople.

Mona had turned the tables for us at her home. I too had managed to get my parents to agree to what I wanted, but not as deftly as Mona had. I immediately updated my parents and Krish about the latest developments. Now, everyone in my house more or less realised the inevitability of the whole issue. All three congratulated me, though I knew my parents were hiding a deep sense of disappointment. "But will she adapt to our culture and food?," my father asked. "We will not tolerate any non-vegetarian food in our house." I assured him she will, and yes, there will be no non-vegetarian food in the house.

My mother now posed another practical question: "But how will all of us now adjust in this small house? Tomorrow Krishnan will also get married and............". I interrupted her, and said: "Amma, because this is a cross-cultural marriage and there is also a space constraint, we will stay in a rented place close by. That will also give you, *Appa* and Mona some time and breathing space to get used to one another." "Yes, that is sensible," my father seconded. "But now I have to explain to all our relatives why we agreed and why Krishnan is not married yet......," my mother started mumbling. In such situations, I could always count on Krish. He never cared for what others had to say. "Why are you bothered about that?," my brother blurted out. "Do they ever consult us for anything?" "I agree," my father said, finally displaying a sense of broad mindedness befitting the times we lived in.

Everything seemed to be falling into place. But there was one more hurdle to cross and its name was Mr Anand Bhatia. My life's most important 'interview' was fixed for late evening the next day. I was many times more nervous than at the time of the many job interviews I had attended. But one thing was reassuring, Mona's presence by my side during the 'interview'.

CHILLY PAPAD

My Life's Most Important Interview

Mr Anand and his family stayed close to Mona's house. "He has three sons aged between 19 and 10. All nice boys, and aunty too is a sweet lady," Mona said, as we arrived at the Bhatia family's doorstep and she rang the bell. Her aunty greeted us with a warm "hello" and a warmer smile, and ushered us into their simple 2 BHK apartment.

Mr Anand's height was 5'8 and his complexion was not as milk white as Mona, but I guessed in his younger days would have passed off as a stud. He looked intelligent and studious. He seemed formal, probably wanting to build the mood for the interview, which I started to feel would be more like an investigation.

After the customary greetings and comments about the climate – discussing climate I feel is always a great way to break the ice – the interview, ah! I mean investigation, ah! ha! I mean the interrogation started:

Mr Anand (sitting stiff to my right in a single sofa with crossed legs, with his gentle wife sitting across him in a chair - his sons had been packed off somewhere I think as they were not around): So you want to marry our daughter Mona?

Me (with Mona sitting next to me): Yes

Mr Anand: Why?

Me: Because I love her, rather we love each other and feel we are a right fit for each other.

Mr Anand: That is a politically correct answer.

Me (a little irritated): Ah…that is the truth sir.

Mr Anand: Have you had any girl friends in the past?

Me: No

Mr Anand: How come you like Mona?

Me (with a slight smile): Well, I don't think there is any logic to it.

Mr Anand: Your parents are happy about this?

Me: Initially they were not, but are now ready for the match.

Mr Anand: Why they were not ready?

Me: Well, people in India don't easily accept inter-caste marriages.

Mr Anand: Then how did you convince them?

Me: I told them I will not marry Mona if they are not ready, but then I will not marry anybody else too, and that I will move out of the city.

Mr Anand (a little surprised): But that is blackmail.

Me (I could sense Mona getting a bit edgy): Not really. It was just a communication of intent.

Mr Anand: I don't believe that. You youngsters cannot be taken on face value. I know what you are…..(I interrupted him)

Me (politely but firmly): Sir, you can ask me whatever you want, but I do not appreciate anybody questioning my integrity.

Mr Anand was taken aback and loosened his crossed legs. I kept my gaze on him as I decided not to let my guard down. I could see Mona bury her face in her palms, as she could not take the tension anymore.

Mr Anand (a little uneasily): Okay, okay….what is your salary?

Me: Take-home Rs 30,000/-

Mr Anand: You think you will be able to give Mona the lifestyle her father is capable of? She is used to living very comfortably.

Me: No, but I am sure Mona is prepared for that.

Mr Anand (carefully choosing his words): Please don't misunderstand me. You know Mona is like my daughter too and I know she is used to a certain comfort. That's why I asked.

Me: Your concern is valid sir. But with God's grace I should be able to improve my financial condition, and in any case she is a working professional too.

Mr Anand: Your parents will allow her to work after marriage?

Me: That will purely be her decision. In any case, my parents will not mind that.

Mr Anand: Who else is there in your family?

Me: My elder brother. He is elder to me by four years

Mr Anand: Is he married?

Me: No.

Mr Anand (He almost sat up): No?

Mr Anand: How big is your house? Is it your own house? Will you stay with your parents after marriage?

Me (to the point, one by one): 1 BHK, it is my parents' house, we will rent a place after marriage, as once my brother gets married, the house may prove small for all of us to stay in.

Mr Anand: Why is he not married as yet? Any problem? I mean.....

Me: I got it. No, everything's fine with him. The search for the right match is on.

Mr Anand: Any other property in Mumbai or in your village? By the way, where do you belong to?

Me (I wanted to say Mumbai, but stopped myself): No sir, my father has only this house. We sold off our ancestral property some years ago. Our family belongs to Kaladaikurchi in Thirunalvelli district. I have visited that place only once in my life as a child (basically I did not want any more questioning regarding my village as I felt that would expose my lack of respect for my roots).

Mr Anand: Any other asset, like jewellery.....?

Me: I am not aware sir.

Mr Anand: You smoke?

Me: No

Mr Anand: You drink?

Me: No.

Mr Anand: Not even beer?

Me: No

Mr Anand (with a light giggle): Then how do you live boy? (I just smiled and stayed quiet. I had noticed he definitely smoked, as his lips were slightly black, but maybe not inside the house, I thought).

Mr Anand (recovering his poise): How will Mona adjust to your culture?

Me: I will help her out

Mr Anand: Anything you want to know? (it almost sounded like the last question from a job interview)

Me: Do we have your blessings Sir?

Mr Anand (got up from the sofa – forcing me to get up too – hugged me lightly, and gave out a light laugh): Of course, of course, welcome to the family. (then looking at Mona said): "Tha... sutta...chokra...aa..."

I grew perplexed. Mona smiled and said: "He said Thamam *sutho chokro aahe*, which means you are a good boy." I was relieved as I wondered why he was mentioning *sutta*, which means cigarette in Mumbaiya Hindi. "*Vaazhga Sir Vaazhga. Okkarunga* (Live long, sit down)," Mr Anand effortlessly shifted to Tamil. "Thank you sir. Your Tamil diction is much better than mine," I said. He smiled back a little embarrassed.

The rest of the evening went off smoothly as we indulged in small talk and some delicacies. After a while, his sons also surfaced and he introduced me to them as their to-be brother-in-law.

But the most important moment of the evening was when he called up Mr Punjabi in front of us and communicated his views about me to him. "Do not worry. Our daughter will be happy," he said, bringing about a huge smile on Mona's and my faces.

FRIED PAPAD

From Fire To The Frying Pan

Things had dramatically turned around. From our houses being on fire, they were now getting ready to place their frying pans to feed us. Soon enough, on the appointed day, Sunday, and at the appointed time, I was at the doorstep of Mona's ground floor home about to ring the bell. I had to walk half a kilometer from the main gate as Mona lived in a large colony which I guessed housed at least 250 flats. I rang the bell and Mona opened the door to welcome me with a warmth and smile that floored me yet again. I felt like hugging her, but behaved myself. "Don't bother to remove your shoes," she said. This was just the beginning of the many differences I would now encounter in our cultures. If anybody entered our house without removing his shoes or slippers, my parents, in not so polite a tone, would ask him to go out, remove them and then come in.

Mona was dressed in a simple T-shirt and jeans, while I was wearing an attire that suggested I had to go to work after lunch. I stepped into a large hall with tastily decorated walls and exquisite marble flooring. It was a 3 BHK apartment and I could immediately make out the financial gap and living standards between our two families. Often, in an inter-community marriage, issues of culture are a camouflage for the gap in the standard of living. After all, doesn't money influence our culture and habits too?

Mona's mother was sitting on the sofa and Mona took me to her. She was a stout but simple lady, and her persona did not quite fit in with the décor of the room. "Namaste aunty," I said, with folded hands, bowed to touch her feet, and then sat on a sofa opposite hers. She probably felt embarrassed at my gesture of touching her feet, but did not object, maybe because she felt too shy to even communicate. She tried to be warm to me, but I could notice she was still coming to terms with what was happening. Soon enough, Mona's bubbly sister Pinky arrived and shook hands with me.

Mona went inside to fetch her father. Mr Punjabi soon arrived dressed in a white shirt and a white trouser. I wondered whether he was Bollywood star Jeetendra's cousin. He was 6 feet tall with semi-white hair, which was drawn equally on both sides. Both Mrs and Mr Punjabi were milk white. So no wonder both their daughters also shared that complexion. I got up and bowed to touch his feet, but he immediately stopped me and hugged me tightly, saying, "In our community the son-in-law is not allowed to touch our feet." This way, he immediately put me at ease. It was evident he had fully accepted our alliance.

In India, even in inter-caste marriages, one thing is common – the respect for the son-in-law. It probably stems more from ensuring the security of their daughter, who has to sacrifice her family to embrace another, than from a sense of respect that naturally comes for the words 'husband' and 'son-in-law'. This respect is not just an attitude, it is steeped in the Indian tradition, making son-in-laws I feel more important than what they actually are. But anyway, son-in-laws don't complain and I wasn't complaining either. This was just the beginning of the process of being made to feel 'special'. The best part of this was that my academic or professional skills had nothing to do with it. Just being born a man and deciding to get married bestowed on me that 'special status'.

Mr Punjabi enquired about my parents and asked when they could visit them for lunch and discuss matters further. "Uncle, they would like to meet Mona first," I said. "Of course." "Also uncle," I said haltingly, "they are expecting that you and aunty will come home first to discuss the formalities." "Don't worry about that. I will speak to them on phone today itself and convince them to come to our home first." I didn't offer any further comments as I now wanted the *samdhees* (the respective parents of the bride and bridegroom are called as *samdhees*) to sort things out amongst themselves.

Soon Mona arrived with two bowls, each with a fair sprinkling of almonds and cashewnuts, and a glass of water. Soon after, she arrived with a glass of orange juice too. "Have Sri. Don't feel awkward. This is your house too," Mona said. Uncle picked up the bowls and urged me to have some almonds and cashewnuts. He also picked up the glass of juice and gave it to me. I felt touched by his hospitality and care. This was just the beginning of the pampering I was to receive as a *naathi* (the sindhi word for son-in-law, which almost sounded like naughty when I first heard it). As I sat admiring the decor of the house, uncle spoke again. "Your parents are fully ready for the alliance I hope." "Yes absolutely. They want to meet Mona first and then speed up the process. Can I take her home with me today?" "Sure."

Through my stay at Mona's house, uncle was courteous, Pinky was sweet, aunty was quiet and Mona was assured. It was evident aunty was a simple homemaker who generally kept to herself and did not speak much. Mona took me around the house and showed me some of Pinky's and her's childhood photos. Then she treated me to some amazing deep fried stuff called *Dal Pakwan*, which I have got hooked on to ever since. This they had ordered from outside, but while it added to your calories in an instant, it tasted the world. It was so heavy that dinner could be easily forgotten. But some interesting South Indian eateries awaited us at home as I informed my parents that I was bringing Mona along.

Mona dressed herself up in a light green saree to come home with me. I could sense that she was not comfortable wearing sarees, but felt that would be the best way to present herself in front of her to-be in-laws. I took leave of the Punjabis, but as I was leaving her mother gave me a sweet box, and her father handed over an envelope. I resisted taking the envelope, as it had money in it. But I could not resist for long, as uncle with folded palms said: "Please take it. This is our culture. You have come to our home for the first time. Also Mona *beta*, once you are there, call me from your mobile. I will speak to Srikkanth's father."

With time, I realised it was a futile exercise refusing to take money from Sindhi relatives, as they found one or the other reason to thrust a few notes into your pocket. The son-in-law status obviously was a great asset. Sindhis had to struggle a lot for money post partition as they had to leave palatial homes and set businesses/jobs to cross the border. But in a few years time they established themselves as rich businesspeople across the length and breadth of the country and spread out all over the world. As my interaction with them increased, I realised abundance as a concept was very close to their heart, and money was their best spokesperson of love and respect.

Soon, we lovebirds boarded a cab. The one deep impression I gathered after leaving Mona's home was that I was getting associated with a family which believed in living abundantly, both in terms of money as well as emotions. Her mother, though spoke little, was kind and her father I thought was an absolute gem. He had totally transformed his attitude for the sake of his daughter's happiness, and obviously Mr Anand's report had a huge influence on his behaviour.

"Did Anand uncle speak to your father again after we left his home?," I asked Mona. "Yes. He was all praise for you. He said you are a very nice and straightforward person and I'll be very happy with you. That lifted a great burden from my father's heart." "But my God, he should be in HR. I don't know how he became an engineer," I said, relieved that I would no longer be subject to any questioning from him.

Now it was time for me to ring the door bell of my house. My brother opened it enthusiastically; just as he was about to make way for our entry, my mother furiously stopped us from entering the house. She went in and soon arrived with a plate filled with red-coloured water (it was *kumkum*, that is, red vermillion, mixed with water) and a small *diya* (lamp lit with wick and oil). She asked Mona and me to remove our footwear, instructed Mona to stand to my right and not my left, as henceforth she was to be my right hand. She circled the plate with the *diya* thrice in front of us and then asked us to enter the house. As we sat down, my mother explained to Mona: "It is our tradition to welcome a new member into our family this way, and also a way to drive away evil forces from your and Srikkanth's lives." I could see Mona was touched. My father was already sitting on the sofa wearing a spotless white shirt and white dhoti. I was happy the two *samdhees* had inadvertently found a 'white' synergy.

Once we all were settled, Mona rose to touch the feet of my parents. My brother expectantly rose too as he wanted to flaunt his chronological superiority, but Mona soon returned to her seat without obliging him. "Later, we will teach you how to do *namaskar* in our tradition," my father told her. For the moment, my parents accepted her way of seeking blessings.

Soon, my mother brought a glass of water for all of us in a tray. Before Mona picked up her glass, she noticed the way we all drank water. Unlike their family, we did not believe in sipping water. We poured it into our mouth. Having noticed us, she too tried to do the same, and spilt some water on her dress. "Don't bother. You drink your way," I told her. "Yes, yes, be comfortable," my father joined in.

Both Krish and me were brought up to believe that sipping and drinking – be it water, tea or coffee – was not a good habit. We also were trained never to eat something already bitten by somebody as it was considered unhygienic, whereas amongst Mona's family members I noticed they sipped and also freely dipped into each other's dishes. But I had not practiced this rule whenever Mona and me ate together – for I had heard that when you eat from each other's plate, your love increases. So, this was a new Sri for her – adhering to traditions within the family environs – and the beginning of an induction program into a Tamil Brahmin Iyer family. She did however ask me later: "Sri, how can you quench your thirst without sipping water? Make it a habit. It feels divine." At Mona's house, I sipped the juice, for it felt awkward to drink it our way.

Soon, deep fried medu vada with sambar and chutney arrived. It was the day of synergies – white clothing and deep fried stuff – but with water-drinking style being a distinct demarcator. "Mona, please have some more vada. Be comfortable," my parents urged her, as we all indulged in small talk.

My mother also served us piping hot South Indian filter coffee. Mona was fascinated by the tumbler from which we drank the coffee. She watched in awe how my parents poured the coffee from the tumbler into the *davara* (Tamil word for metal saucer) and back into the tumbler so that they could cool it and pour it into their mouths. Mona of course simply relished the coffee – by sipping from the tumbler.

I showed Mona around our small 1 BHK apartment. After having visited her 3 BHK home, mine seemed like a model that builders put up at the time of construction. But there was one significant difference. Our house, unlike hers, did have a balcony, and as we stayed on the fourth floor, it presented a nice view. Mona chuckled eagerly, and it was always nice to see her smile.

My parents and brother did their best to make her feel comfortable. My father, not given to praise so easily, finally conceded one, that too in front of his to-be daughter-in-law. "I must say my son has made the right choice. From our side we are happy for all of us," he said. Mona, feeling a little shy and quiet by her standards – understandable of course – smiled at me with approval, almost suggesting that

I had made the right choice, whether she had made one was yet questionable!

Soon, my father was on the phone with my to-be father-in-law. "Good evening Mr Punjabi. *Aapka beti bahuth achchi hai (your daughter is very nice)*," he said in Hindi. Both the fathers exchanged pleasantries. Mona's father, as he had declared, convinced my father to come with family to his house for lunch to take matters further. They agreed to meet the next Sunday – the Sunday sequence was indeed unrelenting.

Even as we were digesting the Sindhi-Tamil deep fried combination of Dal Pakwan and Medu Vada, my mother announced it was dinner time. It was only 8 pm. Mona had once mentioned to me that they normally had dinner at only around 10-10.30 pm. "Aunty, I am full. Will come for dinner again," she said with one hand on her stomach. "No, no. You have come to our house for the first time. You must have a little," my mother insisted. Soon enough, the dining table was ready with rice, sambhar, potato curry, rasam, curd and some fried *papad* and *vadaam* – another deep fried stuff made out of rice (a stereotype had been broken. The Punjabis had not served me any *papad*). "Have this first and then I will serve all of you *payasam*," my mother announced. It almost seemed to me that for a change, the mother-in-law was trying to impress the daughter-in-law.

My brother was unusually quiet and stoic – maybe he was under instruction from my father. My father was very courteous towards Mona. As we ate, he made enquiries about Mona's relatives. Her father was the lone child of his parents with few relatives in close touch. Her mother's relatives were very close to them, she said. Mona was treated extremely well by my family and I was thrilled for that. Though she too had over-eaten, she didn't particularly mind that as she was basking under the attention and affection of my parents. They instantly liked her. I wondered why on Earth did they make such a fuss for so long!

As Mona bid goodbye to my family and I geared up to drop her home, it was now time to induct her into the full body-stretched namaskar. My mother once again instructed Mona to stand to my right, and she herself stood to my father's right side. Here we went then, our bodies in full surrender. Mona was now inducted into the full body-stretched namaskar, and she already looked tired. I wondered what awaited her on marriage day, when many of my relatives would take delight in seeing both of us bow in such reverence. But just as I had not come back empty handed from Mona's home, she too received from my mother a silk saree for herself, a box of sweets for her family and a salwar kameez for Pinky. "Go with care," my father said, as I stepped out with Mona to drop her home.

An extraordinary day had come to an end. From bitter discussions and sullen moods, both families had migrated to a feeling of excitement. Once the acceptance is established, prospects of a multi-cultural wedding are always exciting. Soon, Mona's father called and again invited all of us for lunch to his place and also to discuss the way forward.

Lunch was prepared by Mona. I didn't realise what a good cook she was till that day. Besides deep fried and other delicacies, there was also fried *papad*. My brother looked at me and chuckled when the *papad* arrived, with a 'I-told-you' expression on his face. Both families were careful with words and tried to show as much courtesy as possible. Mona's parents had invited a few of their close relatives also to get introduced to us.

Lunch done, my father took the initiative. "Mr Punjabi, we normally match horoscopes before proceeding on an alliance. But as our children have already decided, we do not wish to get into that. But we still would like to conduct the marriage in a traditional way. We have consulted our *Pundit* (*priest*). He has suggested next Thursday as a good day for Mona and Sri's engagement, and January 22nd for marriage," he said. "That is fine with us. We will book a hall and...." "No, no sir," my father interrupted. "In our tradition, the engagement happens at the boy's home. The entire thing is on us. You need to tell me how many relatives will come from your side. The ceremony has to start at 3 pm and finish before 5 pm, as *rahu kaal* (an inauspicious time when auspicious events should be avoided) starts after that." My to-be father-in-law was a little taken aback. *Rahu kaal* and stuff like that was foreign to him. But Mr Anand was also present and he explained to him what it meant, and also that Tamilians did the engagement in the boy's house.

"We will of course go by what you say Mr Iyer, but I will need to see how I can bring along my in-laws. Since my marriage, which was about 30 years ago, they have not drunk even a glass of water at my place. In our culture, we don't consume anything in our daughter's home. That's why they have not come here today. I'll be grateful if you can come along with me to their house after some time. They stay close by." I now realised why Mona's parents avoided coming to our place. My father, I suspected, was counting the number of times and days his in-laws had come and stayed in our house since his marriage. Just for a moment, I think, he wished he had been a Sindhi.

"Sure, we will come with you. But the engagement has to be in our place, and I will personally request them to come. And yes, they cannot go without eating," my father said in an assertive but pleasing tone. The cultural differences were just beginning to emerge. For my parents, it had of course started with the food – chapatis, paneer, dal, etc, whereas our staple diet was rice, sambhar and curry. Chapati and paneer were tiffin items for us, just as north Indians had south Indian food for change and variety.

I could also see that Mona's parents and relatives were extremely courteous. They were also careful not to say anything that would upset the boy's side. They were very warm - on getting

introduced to the male members, all three of us –
my father, brother and myself – were greeted with
tight hugs, something I felt was going to be the norm
in this family. In a Sindhi family, the amount of
hugs you are subjected to in a day, Tamilians would
probably achieve that in a year. Not that Tamilians
are not warm people, it is just the difference in
cultural expression.

Before the engagement day, Mona's family also
consulted their *Pundit*, and January 22nd was
mutually confirmed as the marriage day. From here
on, days started to fly.

The E-Day arrived. The day marked the beginning
of the merger of two cultures. The ceremony started
our way and ended their way, the only difference
being ours lasted an hour and theirs 15 minutes.
Sindhis wrap up ceremonies real fast, I thought.
Mona and I also realised that from now on we had to
be two people to sets of relatives. Each had to learn
to adapt to the other culture. It was fun actually.

A major revolution took place on that day. My
parents achieved in a matter of minutes what Mr
Punjabi could not for so many years. Mona's
maternal grandparents (her paternal grandparents

were no more; both my maternal and paternal grandparents were no more) ate some delicious stuff at their grand-daughter's to-be home. They had to, as they could not upset the boy's side. But they compensated by forcing some crisp notes down my father's pocket, and this time he could not refuse, as eating free would invite a curse on them, they explained.

As we sat eating and chatting away to glory, my father-in-law said he was extremely impressed with the religious touch to the engagement function. "We normally have a ring ceremony couple of days before marriage. Our functions are more social. And when the two families agree on the alliance, we invite the girl to our house and introduce her to some relatives. After that the boy and girl go out for dinner with a couple of close relatives," he told me.

While he was bowled over by our tradition, I was impressed with their no-nonsense style. Sindhis, I thought, really moved fast. They had self-confidence. They did not run to an astrologer to consult. If boy liked girl and vice-versa, and the families liked each other, that was it. It is not that they never consult astrologers, but that is more as an add-on than as something that has a serious bearing on the decision making. "Even the boy's thread ceremony takes place a few days before marriage," my father-in-law added.

Wow!, I thought. In contrast, my brother and me had to stand through a reception on the day of our thread ceremony, as if we were married to each other. This was because our relatives had told my parents that as they did not have a girl child and were therefore saved from major marriage expenses, they should spend lavishly on our thread ceremony. Our thread ceremony lasted a few hours in the morning, followed by an evening reception, with lots of people in attendance, preceded by a few weeks of preparation, and lots of my father's hard-earned money going down the drain. Most importantly, neither my brother nor I lived up to any of the Brahminical practices we were supposed to follow for the rest of our lives, much to our father's chagrin.

"Sindhis seem to be very practical Sir," I told my father-in-law. "No *beta*, we are uncultured. We just want to enjoy. I like your way," he said. However, I felt he had spoken too soon. "Wait till the marriage discussions start," I told him mentally.

MIXED PAPAD

The Great Cultural Revelations

"The marriage ceremony will start at 6.30. Our *pundit* has identified that as an opportune time," my father announced to Mona's Dad. "That's Ok. The reception can be after that," he replied. "Sindhis hold their reception in the morning?," my father asked a bit sarcastically. "No. In the evening." With a twinkle in his eyes, my father broke the earth-shattering news to Mona's Dad: "I meant 6.30 am Mr Punjabi." "What?", my father-in-law almost jumped out of his chair.

Mona's parents and mine met at her home to discuss the marriage preparations. Mona and me were silent spectators. We decided not to interfere in the elders' discussions. Our only brief to them was that the marriage ceremony should be conducted in both Tamil and Sindhi styles.

The discussions however only further exposed the cultural, financial and social divide that existed between the two communities. We hung around the discussions to avert any incident that would set the process back in any way. "Sindhi marriages normally start in the afternoon and the reception is at around 10 pm," my father-in-law said, probably hoping to have the marriage conducted at a decent and earthly hour, when most Sindhis would be wide awake and ready to attend their relative's wedding. "What? Reception at 10 pm?" It was my father's turn to jump out of his chair. "No, no Mr Punjabi. Our receptions end by 10 pm and everyone goes home by 10.30 pm latest," my father spoke with an assertion and liberty that emerged from being a son's father. Mona's father clearly seemed confused, while her mother was a silent observer to the proceedings.

"I want to be frank with you Mr Iyer. We Sindhis are not used to early morning marriages. Being businesspeople, our receptions also start late to provide space to people to go home from work and then come for the reception. But we will do as you say," Mr Punjabi said, careful not to hurt my father's sentiments. Though far ahead in terms of economic status, he carefully chose his words as he was the girl's father. Some things will probably never change in our country. The boy's side will always assume an artificial superiority and the girl's side will always practice grudging humility.

My mother was waiting for her opportunity to contribute to the discussion. She began with a confidence that only comes with assuming the position of a girl's mother-in-law. In contrast, my mother-in-law was a picture of quietude and respect which comes from being the kind of person she was and also from the worry that comes from handing over her daughter to a stranger and an even more strange community. "Our ceremonies will start two days before the marriage. We will need to move into the hall two days before itself. Our close relatives will also join us for those days. We believe in tradition you know. On the first day at the hall, we will do *sumangali puja* (*a ceremony in which only women participate and is conducted compulsorily before every auspicious event in an Iyer family, dedicated to a deceased woman ancestor*), next day would be repeat of engagement ceremony, and then on the last day, marriage and reception. Mona will have to change many sarees in the process. I will tell you exactly how many later," my mother said. To my in-laws it probably seemed more like the prime minister's son's marriage than of a middle class TamBrahm

Iyer. The change of sarees stuff made Mona look at me with an expression which suggested why I could not have been born as Srichand, a Sindhi, than Srikkanth, a Tamilian.

My in-laws heard my parents with rapt attention, but seemed bemused with the whole rigmarole of a Tamil wedding. But they nodded in agreement to everything and diligently took notes, as after all the expenses were going to be all theirs and the pleasure was all going to be ours. For this reason, I wanted a court marriage, but Mona insisted her parents would be against it and that wedding-related expenses were no problem. She wanted to get married without any further complications. Period.

But I could not stop myself from feeling guilty for being one more groom who gets married at his father-in-law's expense without any meaningful financial contribution from his side. However, I did intervene to try and make things simpler. "Uncle, *Amma, Appa,* I suggest that we reduce the whole affair to one day, and that is the marriage day. We can skip everything else. *Amma,* we can do the *sumangali puja* at our home. Let's not complicate things please," I said nicely, but firmly.

After a brief silence that followed, my mother was about to react, but my father reacted before her. "Yes, I agree. This is an inter-community marriage and we should keep it simple," he said, surprisingly supporting me. My father was tradition-bound and was proud of the Tamil culture, but somewhere he was practical too. "There will be too much of logistical headaches and food wastage. Sri is right. If you are okay with it Mr Punjabi, we will finish off the whole thing in just one day. I understand your relatives may not be used to an early morning marriage, but that is something we can't do anything about. We will arrange for a joint meeting between our respective *pundits* and they can discuss how to combine both the traditions," he added. My father-in-law nodded politely in agreement, but I could sense that he was more than delighted at the prospect of having things wrapped up faster.

My mother's expression however suggested she was waiting to get home to give my father a piece of her mind. She felt a missed opportunity in flaunting extensive arrangements in front of her relatives, despite her errant son getting married to a non-Tamilian. She was already peeved with me that I had put my foot down to any matching of our horoscopes, which is almost like a statutory obligation in Tamil marriages. Sometimes I wonder whether every horoscope should have a statutory warning printed on it: Marriages Are Made In Heaven, But Their Horoscopes Must Match On Earth.

"As you please Mr Iyer. But we would like your family and other close relatives to be a part of our pre-marriage socio-religious ceremonies. We have mehendi (the Indian art of appplying *henna* designs on their palms and feet. Interestingly, the groom is expected to find his initial or name included in the design on the bride's palm, which he invariably does. This is considered as confirmation of love between the bride and the groom). We will also have ring ceremony. We also conduct a '*Mata Ki Chowki*' (devotional songs in praise of Mother Vaishnodevi) before a marriage in the family," my father-in-law said, with utmost considerateness and respect in his tone. "Sure," my father responded.

Mona's parents and mine continued to keep in touch for all marriage-related preparations. Meanwhile, Mona and I indulged in some junk food and 'entertainment shopping'. "I will wear this shirt and go to office tomorrow," I said. "No, not tomorrow. You wear this on Monday. You should not wear new clothes on Saturday," Mona said. "What? How does it matter?" "It does. We don't wear anything new on a Saturday," she said. "Okay dear. I will wear it on Monday," I agreed, not wanting to create an unnecessary rift over a piece of shirt. But briefly I worried whether our cultures were likely to clash in other ways too.

We also tried to teach each other a few words from our respective languages. One interesting revelation for me was the words Sindhis used for husband and wife. Husband is called *'goata'* and wife is called as *'zaala'*. When Mona taught me these words, I laughed my heart out, for I could not believe that Sindhis had captured the essence of the husband-wife relationship so accurately. *'Goata'* resonates with the Hindi word *'bakra'* (a scapegoat), whereas *'zaala'* sounds similar to the Hindi word *'jaal'* (meaning trap). This suggests that Sindhi ladies lay a trap for men and make them a goat after marriage. "So, you laid a trap for me! ha, ha, ha," I laughed out holding my stomach tight. A peeved Mona responded by calling me a *'chadiya'*, which in Sindhi means mad (a mad lady is called *'chadi'*). When she told me what it meant, I called her *'paithiyam'*, which means mad in Tamil.

"Okay, tell me, what do you call husband and wife in your language?," Mona asked me. "Husband is called *'aambdiyan'* and wife is called *'pondatti'*," I said. It was now Mona's turn to hold her stomach tight and laugh her heart out. "So, you are my *'aambdiyaan'* and I am your *'pondatti'*. Wow!" Now it was my turn to look peeved. Once one of her funny cousins asked me how to say 'I am going to heaven' in Tamil. *"Naan swargam pogiren,"* I replied. He actually memorised it, and whenever I meet him, he repeats the sentence to me.

Our funny and serious exchanges of Sindhi and Tamil words continued. We realised learning the languages was such a wonderful way of integrating with each other's culture. Many a cultural divide can be bridged simply by appreciating the nuances of each other's language and by learning to speak it. India as a country offers such an amazing opportunity to learn multiple languages. This way, we can not just increase our repertoire, but also attain a higher level of integration with our countrymen. So in that sense a successful marriage between two people speaking two different languages offers an unique opportunity to diversify out of one's comfort zone, and in the process get enriched – linguistically and culturally.

In the period between our engagement and marriage, Mona took me to meet some of her close relatives in Mumbai. I too reciprocated by taking her to mine. In each Sindhi home, I was received with great affection and tight hugs (from the male fraternity only of course), was fed well, and sent off with some gifts and money. Amongst South Indians, a to-be and already son-in-law would get all this minus the hugs and money. Initially, accepting money (which ranged from 500- to 2000-rupee notes) seemed awkward and embarrassing, but I must say I secretly enjoyed it; anyway I couldn't have got out of it. Stubbornly refusing to take it also meant upsetting them. My parents too felt embarrassed receiving expensive gifts and some cash on Diwali day. They also left no stone unturned to ensure Mona was made to feel special on that day. Besides some jewellery, my mother had ordered an expensive saree for her all the way from Chennai. Mona probably wondered whether she was getting married to a community of saree dealers!

A distinct difference I found between us and the Sindhis, and eventually also between us and the North Indians, was in the expression of affection. My Sindhi relatives were physical and loud in their expression of love, whereas my South

Indian relatives treated us lovingly and courteously, but without any of the physical expressions that go with it. They took delight in showering their blessings after we had prostrated in total surrender. In the process, Mona also collected quite a few blouse pieces and sarees, for whom she had had little use till date. She was yet to even transition properly to *salwar kameez*, and here she was being bombarded with sarees and saree-related accessories.

In contrast, her relatives never allowed me or Mona to touch their feet, as I was their son-in-law and Mona as a daughter enjoyed privileged status. In fact, Mona shared with me about one of her male cousins who sought blessings every morning from his parents as well as his younger sisters. "Some of our people are trained to see the Mother Goddess in their sisters," she explained.

The differences seemed to extend beyond life into death too. In our tradition, there is a specific time and day on which you can visit the home where a death has occurred. Sindhis on the other hand organise a social gathering on the third day post death of a loved one in a *Gurudwara* or a hall, where mourners can come and pay their respects. Mona took me to one such *chautha* ceremony in a Gurudwara, where everyone, clad in white, with their heads covered with a handkerchief, paid their respects in silence and solemnity. It seemed simple and convenient. Of course, it is not to say which is better, but simply highlighting the differences.

Mona also took me to a Sindhi cultural program, where they dished out songs dedicated to their deity Jhulelal. There were dance performances, a play dedicated to cultural values and a clarion call by the elders to promote Sindhi language in each home. The younger generation of Sindhis have moved away from Sindhi literature. Many of them can't even speak their language fluently as they are more adept at the local language. As a Tamil, we were brought up to believe in the richness of our culture, arts, music, dance and customs. My parents, like many others of their generation, were not too impressed with my brother and me for not being adept at the nuances of the Tamil language. Having grown up in Mumbai, Hindi became our daily communication language. I realised a generation of Sindhis too were doing their best to keep their cultural traditions alive.

Sindhis are passionate about the worship of Jhulelal. He is considered their saviour. The cultural evening resonated with the words '*Aayolal jhulelal, jaiko choundo jhulelal, sabaneenjo theendo bedha paar*' (*Jhulelal has come; whoever says Jhulelal will do well in life*).

Again, I could see the difference in celebration style. We Tamils are more controlled in our expression of devotion and celebration, whereas Sindhis let their hair down and dance without inhibitions. Mona tried to pull me into the dance ring in front of the stage, but found marrying me was easier than getting me to dance without self-consciousness.

Our honeymoon plans too encountered the cultural and belief hurdle, as my father over-ruled the day and time of our departure due to the inauspiciousness of the *rahu kaal* factor. We had to postpone our plans by two days, which meant exercising self-control would take precedence over initiative.

The great cultural divide got deciphered further in the *mehendi* and ring ceremonies. The ring ceremony was far more social than religious (the *mehendi* ceremony was attended only by my mother and a few of our lady relatives. They came back feeling awed and shocked). My father asked me cheekily why there was a need for another engagement ceremony when the engagement had already been done. "Simply wastage of money," he remarked in typical Tamil style, bringing every aspect of his cost accountant personality to the core.

Drinks flowed freely and food – vegetarian and non-vegetarian - was made available aplenty as my Sindhi relatives danced, sang, danced more and sang more. My father had a tough time refusing drinks to Mona's relatives. To please them, he ended up having the maximum amount of cold drinks in a day in his lifetime. I could feel his irritation at having to be a part of such a gathering, but he kept his composure and left early with my mother and brother after having light dinner. My mother was under instruction not to make any kind of sarcastic comments and keep a low profile. My ebullient brother seemed lost; therefore stayed quiet and formal throughout.

As for me, it was time to get integrated into the song and dance culture. Mona's relatives ensured we also danced to their tunes. I was literally swept off my feet when the arch lights were focused only on Mona and me and we danced to a Bollywood number. Actually, Mona was dancing and I was getting dragged by her. I must have presented quite an embarrassing sight, but her relatives were kind enough to pay me a compliment. Mona did not seem unimpressed, but if she was, she hid it well from me.

I also wondered whether for my Sindhi relatives a ring ceremony was a platform to display their best and trendiest clothing. Mona dressed aesthetically in a mixture of white and green salwar kameez, while I wore a blue shirt and black trouser selected by Mona herself. Mona looked beautiful and many of her relatives attractive. My parents and few close relatives we had invited felt out of place both with the environment as well as with the culture. But they received unbelievable hospitality, which minimised their discomfort.

The *Mata Ki Chowki* was a wonderful occasion for all of us. Our family thoroughly enjoyed the passionate rendition of devotional songs. They initially found it too loud, but eventually got into the rhythm of the music. The atmosphere for an average Tamil Brahmin Iyer on the occasion was nothing short of extraordinary. Mona's relatives danced and sang in great delight as the singer, accompanied by his orchestra, sang a mix of Hindi,

Punjabi and Sindhi songs. It was quite a sight to watch all the Sindhis dance with great joy to songs in praise of their deity Jhulelal. The food, or the *prasad*, though simple, befitting the mood, tasted divine. My father did draw parallels with the devotional troupes in our village and felt both had their unique spiritual flavour.

All the functions simply highlighted one more of the Sindhi trait – do it grand. If you are out to enjoy, then enjoy no holds barred. Whether it meant giving expression to their worldly emotions, or to their spiritual emotions, Sindhis did it in style, and without holding themselves back. Expression through emotions and money seemed to come naturally to them. One could sense that they were a self-made community and the confidence rubbed off on one another. As a community, they bonded well amongst themselves, were flexible and took calculated risks.

The various interactions meant that both families were now comfortable with each other, and all set for the formal merger of cultures to take place on January the 22nd.

MORE THAN JUST PAPAD

The Two-In-One Wedding

The M-Day – January the 22nd – was just a few days away. Both our families now banned us from meeting each other till we moved into the wedding hall a day before our marriage. The excitement was palpable. We kept in touch through phone and social media. Our pictures together and of all the ceremonies were all over Facebook. An additional ceremony called Ganesh Sthapana (invoking blessings of Lord Ganesha) was performed at Mona's home before the marriage day.

I could sense Mona was both excited and sad, for after all she had to move into a new home and family. We had already finalised the rented home we would move into post marriage.

The *pundits* from each other's communities met to discuss the sequence of the marriage. It promised to be a long one, as each *pundit* was to conduct his process as per an agreed schedule. But a systematic and synchronised amalgamation of cultures on wedding day promised to be exciting and an 'integration connoisseur's' delight. Both our families could feel proud of initiating the integration of parts to create a larger and better whole. Through the ceremonial process, two distinct identities of TamBrahm Iyer and Shikarpuri Sindhi were to be integrated to create a unique conscientious combination of cultures.

Our respective families, close relatives and those from outside Mumbai moved into the hall the previous evening as the ceremonies were to start early the next morning.

The M-Day finally arrived. Mona and me of course could not sleep the whole night due to excitement. So we were up before 4 am itself and got ready. But as the early morning Sun began sprinkling its light on the hall's open verandah, I realised many of our Sindhi relatives looked bleary eyed. It seemed as if they had never attended a marriage so early in the morning. I noticed a lot of them sitting with their eyes closed on a chair. I wore a dhoti with no shirt, whereas Mona looked like a traditional Tamil girl in a nine-yard red saree which she found heavier than her whole frame. She invited comments from my relatives like, "she looks so beautiful in the saree", "she looks like a Tamilian; so what if she is a sindhi", etc. "Now you must learn Tamil Mona," one of them commented. I felt bad that my physique, or the lack of it, was being exposed in front of the 500-odd people who were present at the venue. Many of us of course had slept in the hall the previous night. Many relatives had started coming in from 5 am onwards.

"No breakfast for you and Mona. Only after the marriage ceremony is over," my father announced. To be fair to him, he and my mother too stayed away from the breakfast. Mona's parents were also fasting. But this was atrocious because the smell of the typical Tamil wedding breakfast of pongal, idli, chutney and sambhar was extremely inviting. Mona and I anyway took a round of the breakfast hall and found most of my relatives ensconced safely in their chairs with the banana leaves in front of them, waiting for the items to be served. But we found very few relatives of Mona's sitting at the breakfast table. I assumed they were either struggling to get out of bed, or sleeping seated on the chair in the main hall. We both however helped ourselves to some piping hot coffee and reveled in its aroma and taste. Thankfully, we were not banned from having filter coffee, which is an intrinsic part of Tamil culture.

As we were relishing the coffee, suddenly I felt a hand on my shoulders. I turned around and noticed an elderly man wearing a white shirt and black trouser standing. "*Namaskaram mappilai* (greetings son-in-law)," he said in Tamil. "*Namaskaram,*" I replied, bemused. "Sri, this is Batheja uncle, my mother's cousin. He lives in Salem and he speaks better Tamil than you," Mona said. I again realised just how amazingly well Sindhis, who do not have a state of their own, mingle with the local culture, and yet retain their identity. They truly epitomise the national spirit.

My father-in-law once shared with me how post-partition they all had to overnight leave their large home and a flourishing business in Shikarpur in Pakistan and come to Ulhasnagar. "Me, my mother and a few relatives arrived first in the Ulhasnagar refugee camp. Some of our other relatives took refuge in the Chembur camp. In the commotion, my father was left behind and he joined us a few days later. We thought he may have died, but by God's grace he and all our other relatives were safe, and they arrived later. But many of my friends and their families were not so lucky. I have lost

MORE THAN JUST PAPAD

touch with a lot of people who left Shikarpur, as they either died or settled in other parts of India."

"My father started a small wholesale business of plastic items in Mumbai's Masjid Bunder, traveling almost 60 km one way, and I joined a school near our camp. I used to join my father in the shop after school. As the business picked up, my father found it difficult to handle it by himself. So I dropped out of school and joined him in the business full time. Later I ventured into the electronics goods business and by the grace of God we are doing well."

It was a heart-wrenching story of courage, resilience, and the ability to defy extraordinary odds. I was extremely touched by the story and my respect for the community went many notches up. I was happy I was inheriting the legacy of courage, enterprise and resilience in the form of Mona. She too was self-made and carried herself with a confidence that only comes from a tradition of valour. I felt proud that such a person was to be my wife. I also felt proud of myself that I had made such a wonderful choice. As for Mona, by choosing to marry me, she was going to inherit the legacy of sincerity, loyalty and a value system which were nurtured with great care and caution. "Never tell lies, for to hide one truth, you will have to tell many lies. Always earn your money the right way. Never cheat anyone, for what you sow is what you reap," my father advised both Krish and me many times over. These value systems were ingrained in us from childhood, and they stood us in good stead all through our life.

Our marriage was to be solemnised in just a few hours with the Fire God as witness. There was laughter, humour and lots of learnings about each other's culture in the close to three hours that the whole process lasted.

But before the formal marriage ceremony kicked off, an interesting ritual had everyone in splits. As per our custom, on the day of the marriage, the bridegroom 'threatens' to sacrifice *samsara* (worldly life) and go on a *Kasi Yatra* (pilgrimage to the holy city of Benares). Mona's parents had already been briefed about this. As I began to run away with a stick in my hand, as per custom, my father-in-law came running after me pleading me not to take such a drastic step and accept the hand of his wonderful daughter. I know of no one who has ever rejected his father-in-law's pleading, and I was no exception.

The *Kasi Yatra* ritual was followed by Mona and me exchanging garlands raised atop our respective relatives' shoulders. The ritual of me having to pull out a *khajur* (date palm) from Mona's tightly closed right fist was another interesting and revealing moment. This was now a Sindhi ritual. All of Mona's relatives were egging her on to keep her fist closed as tightly as possible. My brother and other relatives, on the other hand, egged me on to keep the *izzat* (self respect) of our *khaandaan* (family) intact. I struggled hard and Mona seemed to be clearly heading towards victory. But just then she loosened her grip and let me take the winner's award instead. It once again showed just how much women give unconditionally and protect the dignity of their husband and other family members. It was just a game, but in that too was revealed the great emotional character of my life partner. I had often seen my mother go out of her way to ensure the three of us got the best of food and comfort, even if that meant putting herself under some strain. Women are truly wonderful selfless souls.

Our family now took over proceedings for the *oonjal* (swing) ceremony. This is conducted with the bride and bridegroom seated on a swing, to drive away evil forces from their lives. A key moment during the ceremony was when my South Indian relatives, my mother included, broke into a devotional Tamil song. Mona's relatives were awestruck by the classical base, melody and voice quality. In our culture, girls from a young age are given training in Carnatic classical music and Bharatnatyam dance. In yesteryears, a prospective bride had to sing in front of her probable in-laws to demonstrate that she was rooted in culture. In our community, it is not uncommon to find many men also with a deep taste for carnatic classical music. My father himself sings reasonably well and can differentiate between the various ragas with ease.

Our Sindhi relatives were however not quite prepared for what was to follow. As our womenfolk got involved in the nuances of their singing, a few of my male relatives also suddenly joined in. One of them was my father's cousin Mr Subramanian from Chennai. The quality of his rendition made him stand out. He astonished my Sindhi relatives with his voice quality and complex rendition of the classical ragas. Interestingly, Mr Subramanian is the Group HR Head of a multinational company. He is vegetarian, a teetotaler, a devout TamBrahm Iyer who never leaves his house without performing the morning *puja* and applying *vibudhi* (ash) on his forehead, before driving off to his office in his expensive luxury car dressed in a full blown suit and tie. Through the day, he rubs shoulders with corporate professionals and conducts himself with great dignity in the mad, bad profit-hungry world. His knowledge of world politics, economics and corporate strategies makes him one of the most sought-after speakers in HR conferences. And here he was singing a classical devotional song, dressed in a white full shirt, white *veshti*, with three layers of *vibudhi* on his forehead. He also makes an annual pilgrimage to the Holy Sabarimala temple in Kerala, for which he fasts for more than a month, grows a beard, wears the tarditional black dress at home and sleeps on the floor despite owning a duplex bungalow with modern amenities. Mr Subramanian is the quintessential TamBrahm Iyer, who lay great emphasis on education, be a corporate in the corporate world, but stay rooted to tradition and customs. Their values help them navigate through the dust and din of the corporate world. The educated ones occupy big positions in companies. The owners trust them with crores of their rupees, but they are happy taking home a fraction of that and leading a life of loyalty, service and contentment. For many, venturing into business is a no-no, for "that is not what we are meant for – that is for the Gujaratis and the Sindhis."

For a while it seemed like a full blown orchestra was on display. Mona looked at me and asked whether I could sing too. "Yes, in the bathroom," I said, and she laughed loud, attracting some uncharitable looks from some of my very tradition-bound relatives, who could not stomach the lack of cultural orientation of their Sindhi daughter-in-law. They probably thought she was laughing at the singers.

As can be seen from Mr Subramanian's example, one of the great aspects of educated middle class Tamil Brahmin Iyer culture is the intellectual-spiritual ability to balance the nuances of the karmic scorecard and balance sheets of companies. We can be extremely traditional in our outlook and behaviour at any one point, and thoroughly professional at another. We are quite comfortable with the combo of a tie on our neck and *vibhuti* (sacred ash) on our forehead while going to office. I have always marveled at our ability to execute our religious duties with the mark of a professional and perform our professional and worldly duties with a dedication that would please the Gods.

TamBrahm Iyers are an employer's delight. They not only work hard and stay loyal, but also provide the organisation with intellectual vibrancy. On that day, January the 22nd, Mona and me were part of an amalgamation process, and the historic moment of our lives was just round the corner.

We finally took our seats near the sacred *havan kund* (fire pit). Our respective families and the *pundits* from both sides took their positions to be part of a process that would not only culminate in a marriage between two people or two families, but between two communities and two diverse cultures, with habits as distinct as the Sun and the Moon. I felt emotional as it was a day that was going to usher into my life a person who would occupy my very consciousness and not just my life. Mona seemed calm, but was intense from inside. For her, it was the end of a journey and the beginning of a new one. Handling one process is difficult, but she had to handle two at the same time – the end as well as the beginning.

The ceremony got under way with both *pundits* effortlessly coordinating the various rituals from both sides. They had chalked out in detail the sequence of rituals, accommodating both the cultures with effortless ease. It was fascinating stuff.

The highest point of the ceremony of course was the moment I formalised my relationship with Mona, who had demonstrated during the ceremonial process that she was another wonderful, selfless soul on Planet Earth, by letting me win a tug-of-palms contest. I was to tie the *mangalsutra* around Mona's neck, who was sitting on the lap of her father, symbolising with how much love and care he had brought up his child. In his eyes I could see both a sense of relief as well as an urging of me to take care of his most precious possession. Mona sat expectantly as my mother handed me the chain which I had to tie around Mona's neck. This chain would mark Mona out for the rest of her life as a married woman, thereby creating a sense of institutionalised security and social status for her. The tying of the *mangalsutra* would mark a definitive and dramatic shift of her identity from just being her doting parents' daughter to being somebody's wife. From Mona Punjabi, she was going to be suddenly transformed into Mona Srikkanth Iyer. It is amazing how women in India after marriage so effortlessly not only give up their parental home, but also their surname, which up until now provided them with their primary identity.

Just as the Tamil musicians were about to raise the volume to celebrate the tying of the *mangalsutra*, our Sindhi *pundit* suddenly enquired whether I wanted to change her first name, as it was the tradition amongst many Sindhis. Immediately, I could hear some of my relatives rattle out names like Sundari (after all, she looks so beautiful in our saree!), Chitra, Mallika, etc. I quickly but politely refused. I said I was happy with the name Mona, not providing any chance for a discussion. Mona herself stayed silent and when I turned down the suggestion, looked at me with gratitude.

The musicians now raised the volume of their *nadaswarams* (*saxaphones of the South*) and *mridamgams* (*drums of the South*). All relatives took their positions to shower flowers on us as I closed in to enact the ultimate act in a Hindu marriage, the tying of the *mangalsutra* around the bride's neck. My nervous hands made a cup around Mona's neck. One of my elder cousin sisters kept a close watch on whether I was locking the chain properly. After a brief struggle, I safely locked the chain around Mona's neck. The sound of the drums and *nadaswarams* reached a crescendo, flowers started falling from above, while tears flowed down from Mona's, mine and her parents' cheeks. After a few moments of emotional release, our relatives began congratulating us, even as the *pundits* urged us to settle down for the next part of the uncompleted ceremony.

The comment of the day of course came from my brother, whose sense of humour was divorced from the sense of timing, so crucial to good, quality humour. Even as Mona and I were recovering from the high emotional state we had experienced just a few minutes ago, my brother, in a voice as loud as the sound of a train horn at midnight commented: "Sri, you only tied the *thaali* (*mangalsutra* in Tamil), but you are now tied to your wife all your life. Mona, don't worry, we also love eating papad. You will get a lot of them," and started laughing in his trademark style, heavily cheered by my male as well as female cousins and other relatives. Some of them even commented: "It is now your turn Krishnan. Learn something from your brother and find somebody for yourself." Mona, though not too amused by my brother's comment, put up a brave face and let out a slight smile.

Post the ceremony, Mona and I were hugged by our Sindhi relatives, whereas our elderly Tamil relatives made us do full body-stretched namaskars as per tradition. This was yet another interesting contrast. We then proceeded for the *Grahapravesh* ceremony at my parents' home, while our Tamil and Sindhi relatives were treated to some amazing South Indian food. We could eat only after the *Grahapravesh*. Reports suggested our Sindhi relatives thoroughly enjoyed the food. There was a break from custom though. Instead of food being served on banana leaves, it was served in plates, as our Sindhi relatives might have struggled to eat otherwise. It does take some basic orientation to eat on banana leaves – which actually are eco-friendly – as retaining the *sambar* and *rasam* as well as the plethora of *curries* within the boundaries of the leaves is an art.

When we came back from the *Grahapravesh*, as per Sindhi custom, we were served food in the same plate. The practice of togetherness had to start from food. We ate slowly and happily fed each other. Lunch done, we had to gear up for the reception. Mona had an appointment at the parlour, while I looked forward to some rest before getting ready for the 'stand and deliver' reception fucntion. But before we could go our ways, something unexpected happened.

A few of Mona's young cousins, with Pinky acting as a leader, came to me and asked whether I recognised a pair of shoes they were carrying. "Yes, it is my reception shoes," I said. "Our dear brother-in-law, you have two choices. Either pay us Rs 50,000/- only (and they stressed hard on the word only) and take it back from us, or stand on stage without your shoes on," they happily announced to loud cheering from Mona's relatives who had gathered around us as if to witness a puppet show. They all said it together; so they must have rehearsed it well. My relatives, on the other hand, seemed more aghast than amused. Their expressions suggested they thought I was marrying a 'family of thieves'. In Sindhi marriages, however, this is a custom. It is a moment the girl's side relatives plan for and eagerly look forward to, simply to add some fun to the proceedings. Flicking off the bridegroom's shoes is a well-planned strategy, which even the bridegroom is aware of. So, the bridegroom's family also tries to safeguard his shoes from the prying eyes of the bride's relatives. But as I was not a Sindhi and we had no idea about such a custom, it was much easier for them to flick my shoes. Mona had purposely not informed me about it. In fact, I later learnt she was party to the 'shoe kidnapping' process.

My parents and brother however were very excited about this. "Sri, remember the number of times you wore my slippers without permission? Now, it is payback time," my father said, and started heartily laughing at his son's predicament. "But I don't have 50,000 now," I told my 'shoe thieves'. "We accept credit card too," one of them shot back, to one more loud cheering from Mona and my Sindhi relatives. "But I am not carrying my card either." "Well, ask for a loan from somebody then." I looked at Mona. "Sorry Sri. I don't have any money either," she said, with a mischievous expression on her face. Her relatives lustily cheered her for standing by them. It was clear the palm date episode was not going to repeat itself. This time, I had to bail myself out.

My brother realised my predicament. He was the one handling all the cash. So he stepped in. "Okay, let us settle for Rs 25,000," he said. "No, no, no. It's 50,000 or no shoes," they all shouted, including, believe it or not, my parents and Mona.

"Krish, give them 50,000. They deserve it. Let them enjoy," my father said. I still can't understand from where my father gathered such abundance mentality and was ready to scarifice Rs 50,000 of his family's hard earned money. Krish pulled out Rs 50,000, which was neatly wrapped in an envelope from his pocket and was about to give it to Pinky. He was carrying about a lac of rupees as cash back-up. But my father-in-law, who was watching the whole episode, quietly stepped in and asked Krish to give only 25,000. Pinky and her cousins tried to keep him out of this, but he refused to budge. They grudgingly accepted Rs 25,000, returned the shoes, broke into a celebratory noise and ran off. It was amazing to see how my father-in-law was keen to save few thousand rupees for my family when he himself was spending lacs on his daughter's marriage.

The reception was pleasant, but uneventful. Our Sindhi relatives participated with gusto in an event whose timing was unusual and unfamiliar to them. It started at 7.30 pm and ended at 10.30 pm, around the time normally Sindhi receptions start. It is not unusual in Sindhi receptions to find a large number of people standing alongside the stage in a queue waiting for the couple to arrive. In Tamil receptions, however, the couple step on stage like disciplined soldiers and await the arrival of the well wishers. Mona wore a simple looking but expensive and nice blue salwar kameez, whereas I got myself into a black suit. A large number of my father-in-law's business associates attended the reception, swelling attendance from Mona's side way beyond ours.

Reception and dinner over, it was time for us to now move towards the hotel for our first night. I had watched in Hindi films the melodrama that precedes a girl's *bidhai* (farewell). But that night I witnessed a scene which ensured I not only do not forget it all my life, but also institutionalised in me the sense of responsibility that comes with separating a lady from her family. Mona's father tried his best to hold back his tears, but her mother and sister were uncontrollable. Mona was the elder child and the soul of the house. Mona did her best to keep her tears in check, and comforted her sister and mother by saying that she was going to be in the same city.

What touched me the most was when my mostly silent mother-in-law, tears rolling down her cheeks, came to me, and with folded hands said:

"My daughter from today is yours. Please take care of her." "I will," I assured, and hugged her. That affectionate moment also made me realise that just as my parents were Mona's, her parents were mine too. I then proceeded to touch the feet of my father-in-law and say goodbye to him. He stopped me from touching his feet and hugged me tightly. All his resistance finally gave way. He broke down and said, "*Beta* I am giving you a piece of my heart. Please take care of her."

In contrast, my parents were excited about welcoming a new member into their family. But they were sympathetic about Mona's parents', sister's and other relatives' feelings. "Mona is our daughter Mr Punjabi. Do not worry about her," my father comforted my father-in-law. I wondered how and when this tradition of a girl leaving her family after marriage started. Maybe one person had to let go to create a union between two families, and the large-hearted women folks always made the sacrifice.

We soon were in the car to go towards the hotel. I put my arm around a sobbing Mona to comfort her. One of my cousins and his wife came with us to lead us into our room. Along the journey, I, who for a while had been fantasising about our first night, realised more strongly that marriage was more than just a union between two bodies. It was a union of two souls. It was a union of two families, and in our case, even two diverse cultures. The sense of responsibility was not only towards each other, it was also towards society – in terms of providing a stable marriage and enhancing the reputation of the institution – and towards creation, by being good and loving parents to our children. Marriage, I realised, was not such a simple process after all. I suddenly developed a deeper respect for all the hue and cry people make about the right match, the right fit, the right proposal, the right family, and all the other rights about marriages in India.

My thoughts were interrupted as our car screeched to a halt outside our hotel. I noticed Mona too had settled down a bit.

Soon enough, we were alone in our room. Both of us sat on the edge of the bed for a while holding each other's hands, tired – emotionally, mentally and physically. Mona moved closer and placed her head under my left arm, as if to find some rest closer to my heart. After a while, I removed my arm from around her neck, lifted her chin, looked deep into her eyes, and said: "I am sorry." Mona got worried and asked anxiously, "For what darling?" "For separating you from your family," I said, in a choked voice. Mona, wiping my tears said, "Don't be silly Sri. I will miss them, but I know I will always be happy with you. I love you." "I love you too," I said, and we both hugged each other tightly.

On that day, the 22nd of January, a new journey had started for two people, representing two different communities from two diverse cultures. Yet, funnily, one thing seemed common. We as a family loved eating papad, and Mona too came from a so-called papad-eating community. Papad had become a lifelong symbol of our relationship. But even as we found comfort in each other's arms, we realised that life for both of us from then on was going to be **More Than Just Papad**.

About The Author

Hariharan Iyer is a seasoned Learning & Development professional with over 25 years of training experience. He is a multi-faceted personality with varied interests – speaking, training, writing and 'bathroom singing'. He is popularly referred to as The Enter-Trainer™ due to his entertaining style of training. He is Founder of Hariharan's School Of Success (HSSE) Education, which is a training organisation (www.theentertrainer.in).

This is his fourth book and the first in the fiction genre. He regularly writes a blog under the name – bolharrybol.blogspot.com. He can be reached on hariharan@theentertrainer.in.